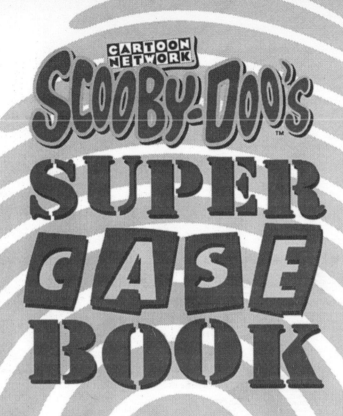

SCOOBY-DOO'S SUPER CASE BOOK

BY VICKI BERGER ERWIN AND SUZANNE WEYN

SCHOLASTIC INC.
New York   Toronto   London   Auckland   Sydney
Mexico City   New Delhi   Hong Kong   Buenos Aires

No part of this publication may be reproduced in whole or in part, or stored in a retrieval system, or transmitted in any form or by any means, electronic, mechanical, photocopying, recording, or otherwise, without written permission of the publisher. For information regarding permission, write to Scholastic Inc., Attention: Permissions Department, 557 Broadway, New York, NY 10012.

ISBN 0-439-40788-5

Copyright © 2002 by Hanna-Barbera.
SCOOBY-DOO and all related characters and elements are trademarks of
and © Hanna-Barbera.
CARTOON NETWORK and logo are trademarks of
and © Cartoon Network.
(s02)
Published by Scholastic Inc. All rights reserved.
SCHOLASTIC and associated logos are trademarks
and/or registered trademarks of Scholastic Inc.
Designed by Louise Bova

12 11 10 9 8 7 6 5 4 3   2 3 4 5 6 7/0

Printed in the U.S.A.

First Scholastic printing, June 2002

CONTENTS

Daphne, Velma, Fred, Shaggy, and Scooby-Doo stood at the end of a dock. "It's so pretty here!" Daphne said with a happy sigh.

The waters of Lake Oscawanna shimmered in the late-morning sun. Trees lined the curving shore and, overhead, white clouds billowed like towering castles in a crystal-blue sky. Three geese glided in for a landing on the dock's railing.

"Perfect," Fred agreed.

Velma nodded. "I can't think of a better place to learn to sail. I'm so glad someone

1

slipped this sailing school advertisement under my door."

She took a folded piece of paper from the pocket of her skirt, unfolded it, and read aloud, "'Breezy Winds Sailing School. Learn the basics of sailing in one week. Enjoy a beautiful lakeside experience with skilled instructors.'"

"Like, at least this will be one place with no monsters, ghosts, or vampires," Shaggy said. He had already rolled up his pants and was sitting with his legs dangling in the water.

Scooby sat beside him, splashing his paws in the water, too. "Rat's right! Ro rysteries rere."

Shaggy saw something floating in the water and reached down to scoop it up. "Yuck," he said. "It's, like, a piece of green rubber or something." He looked around for a trash can, but he didn't see one, so he stuffed the scrap into his pocket.

At that moment, a man in his twenties strolled onto the dock. "Hi, guys," he greeted them. "I'm Breezy Winds, owner of the sailing school. I was so glad you called to sign up for classes."

"We read your ad and it looked like fun," Velma told him.

Breezy smiled at them. "Ready to start?"

"Sure," Daphne agreed. "But are we the only ones taking the class?"

"I like to keep my classes down to four pupils," Breezy replied.

Scooby cleared his throat loudly. "Ra-hem!"

"You mean, like, five," Shaggy corrected Breezy.

Breezy stared uncertainly at Scooby-Doo. Then he shrugged. "Yeah. Five. Whatever you say."

The gang followed Breezy along the shore to where three small boats lay on the sand. "These are called Sunfish," he said. "They hold one to two passengers and have only one sail. I like to start students with these because they're light and easy to learn."

"And they're gorgeous!" Daphne added.

For the next half hour Breezy showed the gang how to put the small sailboats together. They set the mast in place, put in the rudder, and inserted the centerboard. Breezy showed them rope knots, and they learned how to judge which way the wind was blowing.

"All this learning is making me hungry," Shaggy said.

"Me, roo," Scooby agreed.

"You two can eat later," Fred told them as he dragged one of the boats into the water. "I want to try sailing."

"Well, if you hear a loud rumbling sound, that's my stomach," Shaggy grumbled. "Mine and Scooby's."

Breezy assigned Fred and Daphne to share one sailboat. He put Velma on another, and Shaggy and Scooby on the third. "I'll get into my motorboat and join you," he added.

The gang learned quickly and was soon gliding along the lake's surface. "Isn't this great?" Daphne said to Fred as she held the sail line tightly in her hand.

"It sure is," Fred agreed. Velma sailed past them, smiling, and Fred waved to her.

"Hey, Daph, check out Scooby and Shaggy," he said.

Daphne turned and laughed. Scooby and Shaggy's sail flapped back and forth in the wind as they spun in circles. Breezy, in his small motorboat, was going to help them.

Fred, Daphne, and Velma sailed out into the middle of the lake. Breezy soon joined them. "Where's Shaggy and Scooby?" Fred shouted to him.

"I guess they've given up," Breezy shouted back, pointing over his shoulder.

Scooby and Shaggy had taken down the sail and were on their bellies paddling, like two surfers sharing a board. The gang was still giggling at the sight when suddenly their boats began to swirl around in a large circle.

"Jinkies! What's happening?" Velma cried as the center of the swirling water grew dark.

Scooby and Shaggy's boat was caught in the whirlpool, too. The water swept everyone around and around.

"Hey! Surf's up!" Shaggy shouted happily as he and Scooby stood and surfed, riding the waves. But they instantly sat back down when they saw that something was coming up out of the center of the whirlpool. It was something very big and ugly.

"Ronster!" Scooby yelled.

A slimy green lake monster rose up from the swirling vortex. It was nearly twelve feet tall, part frog, part fish, and part human. Its finny arms lashed out, whipping in all directions.

One of the arms knocked Scooby and Shaggy off their boat. "Like, cowabunga, dude!" Shaggy shouted as the spinning water sucked him and Scooby down. In minutes they had disappeared below the surface.

"Shaggy! Scooby!" Velma cried.

"Oh, no!" shouted Daphne.

The hideous lake monster quickly sank down into the water again. As suddenly as it had begun, the lake water stopped spinning.

The gang immediately jumped into the water and began searching for their friends. Fred, Daphne, and Velma dove down deep under the water. They spotted a small light and swam toward it, but the light went out and they were soon lost in darkness.

Fred, Velma, and Daphne managed to swim straight up. They popped their heads above the surface at the same time. Breezy extended his hand and pulled them into his motorboat.

"We've got to find Shaggy and Scooby," Daphne said, wringing water from her hair.

"I have scuba gear and lights," Breezy told them. "Let's go back to shore and get them." He took down the sails on the other boats and towed them as he raced for shore.

When they neared the shore, two horrible creatures appeared on the land. They staggered toward Breezy and the gang, groaning and waving their arms.

"Oh, no!" Fred said. "More lake monsters!"

Breezy cut his speed and approached cautiously. Velma had found binoculars and a remote control in a case under one of the seats. She used the binoculars to study these new creatures. "They *are* hideous," she commented. "But something about them is familiar."

As she continued to watch, one of the creatures clawed at his face. Dark eyes peered out from between its reedy covering.

"It's Shaggy!" Velma shouted.

Breezy picked up speed again and hurried to dock his boat. The gang sprang out and raced to their friends.

"Relp! Relp!" Scooby cried. He was wrapped in so much lake grass that his shouts were hard to hear. Shaggy, too, was wrapped like a mummy in lake grass and reeds.

Velma, Fred, and Daphne pulled apart their friends' wrappings, and in minutes they were free. "What happened?" Fred asked.

"Like, we don't know," Shaggy told them. "We went under and it was too dark to see. Then somebody jumped us, wrapped us in this stuff, and put us into some kind of box. The next thing we knew we were being dumped out here."

Breezy Winds walked up to them. "You've discovered my secret. This is why you were the only ones here today. People don't want to be the victim of the lake creature, so no one signs up for my classes."

Shielding her eyes from the sun, Velma gazed down the shoreline. Sailboats were taking off from a nearby dock. "Why aren't *those* people scared to go out?" she asked Breezy.

He shrugged. "That's another sailing school. They don't seem to be bothered by the creature."

The gang looked at one another. "Let's go have a talk with the owner of that sailing school," Fred suggested. They hurried down to the next sailing school and were greeted by a pretty young woman.

"Hi, I'm Gale Winds. Welcome to my sailing school," she said. "Care for a lesson?"

"You must be related to Breezy Winds," Daphne observed.

The woman made a face of disgust. "Wish I wasn't. He's my little brother. He wants to be my partner in this business, but I won't let him. He's too much of a goof-off. He'd want me to do all the work while he ran off

9

and did his sculptures. What he really wants is to be an artist."

The gang told her about their terrifying encounter with the lake monster. "Breezy says this thing doesn't bother your students," Fred added. "Why do you think that is?"

"I have no idea, but it's his problem, not mine," Gale replied. "Now, if you'll excuse me, I have a sailing class to run."

"Where are Scooby and Shaggy?" Daphne asked.

"There they are," Velma said, pointing toward the road that circled the lake. "And they have company."

Scooby and Shaggy stood outside a hot-dog truck, eating one hot dog after another. As they ate, they spoke to a man who wrote everything they said down on a pad. Fred, Daphne, and Velma hurried to join them. They arrived just in time to hear Shaggy say, "The monster was, like, horrible, man. It grabbed us and flung us around with its icky, slimy, disgusting webbed hands and . . ."

"And what?" the man prodded excitedly.

"And I'm out of hot dogs," Shaggy told him. "I don't remember things well when I'm starving."

"Ri reed ra rot rog, roo," Scooby added.

"Scoob needs another one, too," Shaggy translated for the reporter, who hurried to the truck to buy more hot dogs.

"What's going on?" Fred asked Shaggy.

"Oh, like, this reporter guy showed up and wants our story. He says this is the break he needs to become a top reporter. So, Scoob and I were happy to talk to him . . . for a price, of course."

Velma scratched her head. "How did he know about what happened?" she wondered aloud. "We were the only ones out there when the lake monster showed up."

"Remember, this has happened before," Daphne said.

"Or maybe we weren't the only ones there," Fred added.

"Shaggy, you have relish on your cheek," Daphne said.

"Zoinks! Like, how embarrassing!" Shaggy

replied. He pulled a tissue out of his pocket to wipe it up. The piece of green rubber he'd found in the water earlier fell out.

Fred picked it up and studied it. "Where did you find this, Shaggy?" he asked. Shaggy told him. "I think it's time we came up with a plan," Fred said slowly. "First, let's change into our bathing suits and tell Breezy we'll be taking a late-night canoe ride."

Daphne held the flashlight as Fred paddled at the front of the canoe and Velma paddled in the back. It was dark and quiet. The only sound was the crunching that came from Scooby and Shaggy munching on Scooby Snacks as they sat in the middle of the canoe.

Suddenly, the dark water began to churn. The canoe spun as the water swirled. "Zoinks! I don't like this!" Shaggy said, his mouth full of Scooby Snacks.

In the darkness, the creepy figure of the lake monster began to rise. Its finlike arms flew out from its side, seeking its next victim.

"Now!" Fred shouted. Daphne, Shaggy, and Velma stood and threw a large fishing net over the monster's head. The canoe rocked dangerously as they pulled the creature toward them.

"We've got it!" Daphne cried. The monster was about to topple over completely.

"Whoa!" everyone yelled at once as the canoe flipped. The gang came up out of the water and saw the monster floating lifeless in the net. Velma, Fred, and Daphne dove down and came up holding a man in a scuba outfit. Fred pulled off his face mask and the culprit was revealed.

Do you know who was responsible for the lake monster? Turn the page to find out if you're right!

"Breezy Winds!" Daphne cried. She turned toward the others. "We were right!"

The gang figured it was Breezy based on the clues they'd collected. The piece of green rubber floating in the water told them that the lake monster wasn't real. They also knew that Breezy Winds owned scuba equipment, which meant he was able to go underwater whenever he wanted. Velma also saw the remote control on the boat. What would Breezy need a remote control for?

The gang had other suspects besides Breezy. Gale Winds's sailing school was competition for her brother. She might want to create a monster to put him out of business. The reporter might have made up the big story to boost his career. After all, he seemed to know about everything that was going on.

But Breezy Winds had the means and the motive. As a sculptor, he was able to create the monster out of rubber. He used the remote to activate the monster. His monster was a rubber sculpture attached to a large fan on an underwater platform. When Breezy turned it on with his remote, the fan swirled the water. It also turned on a lift, like the kind used to hoist cars. That brought up the monster.

When Scooby and Shaggy were accidentally sucked under, Breezy quickly donned his scuba gear and grabbed them. To keep them from seeing the setup below, he wrapped Scooby and Shaggy in lake grasses and reeds. He then zoomed back to shore with them and left them there.

What was his motive? Gale tipped off the gang when she said Breezy wanted to be part of her business. He opened his sailing school to show her that he could run a sailing school on his own. But it didn't do well, and he wanted it to seem like it wasn't his fault that he was going out of business. He set up the monster so Gale would feel sorry for him and think his business was ruined through no fault of his own. He called the reporter and left the ad for the gang so his story would make headlines Gale was sure to see.

15

"I'm sorry, you guys. And especially you, Gale. Is there any way I can make it up to you?" Breezy asked.

"That's okay, Breezy," Velma said.

"Like, hey," Shaggy said. "That lake monster was pretty awesome. I bet people would pay to come out and see it."

"You're right. We could take them out on my sailboats and charge them," Gale said to Breezy.

"Does that mean we're partners?" Breezy asked.

"Partners," Gale agreed.

"Rooby-rooby-roo!" Scooby cheered.

"Like, Scoob, I don't know," Shaggy said. "It's been a long time since I rode a horse. I'm not so sure I want to do this."

Scooby nodded and looked around nervously at the horses in the stable.

"Oh, don't be chicken," Velma said, leading her horse out of its stall.

"Don't remind me of chicken," Shaggy complained. "I haven't had anything to eat since my after-lunch snack."

"That was only a half hour ago," Velma reminded him.

"Really?" Shaggy asked. "It seems much longer."

Fred and Daphne walked in, leading their horses. "Ready?" Daphne asked. Her uncle's friend Happy Trails had invited them to ride horseback at his stable. "What's taking so long?" she asked.

"Shaggy's scared," Velma told her.

"I am not," Shaggy protested. "Hop on, Scooby. We'll show them what real cowboys look like." Scooby backed up, then ran to the rear of the horse and leaped on.

Happy Trails came into the stable. "Ready for the best trail ride you ever took?" he asked with a big grin.

"We're ready," Fred replied as he stepped into his horse's stirrups. Velma and Daphne climbed into their saddles and were ready to ride.

Happy was about to get on his horse when a man in a suit charged into the stable. He held a cell phone in one hand and a large briefcase in the other. "One minute, Trails!" he cried. "You're not taking any more rides out of my stable."

"*Your* stable?" Happy shouted. "You're a cheater and now you want to be a thief!"

As the two men argued, the gang got an idea of the problem. Four nights earlier, Happy had been in a card game with this man, Stu Jones. He had bet his riding stable and lost. But, minutes after losing, he discovered Stu Jones had cheated.

"I'll never honor a bet made with a cheater!" Happy declared angrily.

"I want to knock this stable down and make a computer graphics center," Stu Jones said. "People will flock here to have my company do computer art for them. I won this stable so I could do that, and I'm going to do it."

Ignoring Stu, Happy just rode out of the stable and waved for the gang to follow him. As the gang followed behind him, they watched Stu get into his car and race off, spraying dust and rocks.

They were about to head into the forest when a woman wearing a cowboy hat hurried out of the office building beside the stable. "Happy," she said, "I just now got an offer to manage a big hotel in town. They need my reply."

"Tell them no," Happy replied.

The woman stomped her foot. "I only stay and work in this crummy office because you keep saying we're getting married. When are you going to set the date?"

"You can't rush these things, Ida," Happy told her.

Ida turned red with anger. "I hate this stable, Happy!" she shouted. "I wish it was shut down and we could go live in town like normal people!" She stormed away, back to the office. When she slammed the door behind her, the building seemed to shake.

"Ida and me've been engaged for twelve years," Happy explained. "As I said, you can't rush these things."

Happy clicked for his horse to move forward. The gang followed him onto a trail leading into the woods.

They rode for hours, and by the time they headed back toward the stable, the sun was beginning to set.

"Jinkies!" Velma suddenly cried. "What's that?"

The gang and Happy had to pull back on their reins as a wild white horse reared up in front of them. It neighed, then galloped toward them.

"Yikes!" Shaggy shouted as the white horse chased him and Scooby. It came closer and closer, gaining on them every second. Shaggy and Scooby grabbed a low-hanging branch and scrambled up the tree just as the horse was about to overtake them. Their horses picked up speed and cantered away. The white horse leaped up at the tree and sailed through the branches before it disappeared from sight.

"Wow!" Daphne said.

"Do you know that horse?" Fred asked Happy.

"I'm afraid I do," Happy told him. "It's the Nightly Mare. She started appearing out of nowhere just three months ago. People around here say a mare was killed in a stable fire years ago. They believe she's come back to haunt my stable because she thinks it's where she died."

"Uh, like, I hate to bring this up," Shaggy said as he and Scooby climbed down from the tree, "but those folks might be right. That horse didn't leave any hoofprints."

The gang gathered around. Shaggy was right — no prints.

The gang didn't have time to think about it for long, though. The sound of neighing filled the forest. "My horses!" Happy cried. "Someone's freed them all!"

He kicked his mount's flanks and galloped after the horses. Fred, Daphne, and Velma tried to help him, too. Shaggy and Scooby took the opportunity to stop and eat some blueberries they'd found on a nearby bush.

It took Happy and the gang two hours to chase his horses back to the stable. Finally, they were able to ride back and dismount.

"Listen, kids," Happy said to them as they washed down their horses. "Daphne's uncle told me you solve mysteries. That's really why I invited you all here. That Nightly

22

Mare keeps showing up and scaring away my customers. It appears without any warning. There's only one time I know for sure that it will come. It's been outside the office every midnight for the last three nights. Could I convince you to stay and figure out what's going on?"

"You can count on us," Fred told him.

"Thanks," Happy said. "I'd better get to the office and talk to Ida — find out if we're still engaged." With a wave, he hurried inside the office.

Velma looked down and saw something on the ground covered in dirt and hay. It was a gray plastic letter *T*. Daphne joined her. "What is it?" she asked.

"It looks like a letter from a computer keyboard," Velma answered. "I wonder what it's doing here in a stable."

A stable hand came in, leading one of the horses back into its stall. "Do you use a computer here in the stable?" Velma asked him.

The young man shook his head. "The only computer is in the office," he answered.

Fred joined them. "Have you seen any of the strange things happening around here lately?" he asked the stable hand.

The young man snorted with laughter. "Are you kidding? That Nightly Mare is definitely haunting the place."

"Do you like working here?" Daphne asked the young man.

"It's okay. But I'm an O'Dool. Randy O'Dool. If my dad hadn't lost this stable in a card game, it would be mine by now." Talking about this seemed to upset him and he quickly brought the horse into its stall. When he came out again, he wouldn't even look at the gang.

"I think we should split up and look for clues," Fred suggested. "Daphne and I will look around by the office. Shaggy and Scooby, you two poke around the horse stalls. Velma, you check out the road. We'll meet back here."

The gang did as Fred suggested. Shaggy and Scooby walked in and out of every stall. They saw horses eating hay. "Hungry as I am, Scoob, I don't think hay is for me," Shaggy commented.

Scooby didn't reply. He'd found a bucket filled with oats and grains. He ate it noisily, shoving big pawfuls into his mouth.

Shaggy found some apples and carrots in a pail. "I don't think the horses will mind sharing," he said as he chomped into an apple.

Scooby began to choke, clutching his throat.

"I'm coming, buddy," Shaggy shouted. He grabbed Scooby around the waist and pressed hard. He did it three times. On the third try, something shot out of Scooby's mouth. It bounced off the stall wall and dropped right at Scooby's feet.

Shaggy bent down and picked up the object Scooby had been choking on. It was a black metal piece that fit into his palm. "It might be, like, a clue," Shaggy said.

After an hour, the gang met to go over their clues. Shaggy showed them what they'd found in the horse oats. "It's a battery," Velma said. "A laptop computer battery. I also found a clue. Out on the road I discovered tire tracks in one of the stable's pastures. It looked like someone had driven off the road into the pasture and parked the car right there."

"It's time to set a trap," Fred said. The gang huddled together while Fred laid out his idea.

Just before midnight, the gang gathered in the open space by the stable and office. Happy joined them. The Nightly Mare appeared right on schedule. It reared up and whinnied.

Then it turned green, red, and striped. Its head went to the right, while its legs split off its body and moved in four opposite directions at once. After that, it began to bark like a dog. Finally, it fuzzed with gray TV static and fizzled out.

"What happened to the ghost?" Happy asked.

Velma held up a piece of black plastic that looked like a remote control. "This happened to it!" she said. "It's a signal scrambler. I've scrambled the signal of the holographic beam coming from . . ."

Fred and Daphne stood at either side of a five-foot-tall wooden shed built to hold garbage cans. "It's coming from in here," Fred said as he and Daphne flipped back the lid.

Slowly a person rose up from the shed. It was a person Happy Trails knew well.

Do you think you know who was responsible for the Nightly Mare? Turn the page to see if you're right!

27

Stu Jones used the laptop computer he carried in his briefcase to work the holographic beam he kept in there. The beam projected a three-dimensional image of a wild white mare wherever he wanted it. He could make it move using the graphics program in his computer. He also took advantage of the distraction to do mysterious things like freeing the horses.

Stu hoped that by scaring Happy Trails and ruining his business, he could get his hands on the property, which he planned to turn into a highly profitable computer graphics center.

The gang figured this out by collecting the clues. Velma found the keyboard letter and Scooby choked on the computer battery. This told them that a computer was involved. (When the gang inspected Jones's computer they found that, indeed, the letter *T* was missing.)

The kids also had reason to suspect Ida and Randy O'Dool. Both had motives for wanting the stable shut down. And Ida used a computer, but not a laptop that required a battery. But most important, neither of them had the means to create the Nightly Mare. Stu Jones's knowledge of technology and computer art made him the only suspect who could have made the horse's image. And finally, when Velma saw the tire tracks in the field, it told her that someone had left, then sneaked back into the field. Stu Jones was the only one who'd driven out.

In the end, Stu Jones was arrested for endangering Happy's horses. Happy married Ida. He also played cards with young Randy O'Dool and bet half the stable, which Randy won. The gang suspected he might have done this on purpose just to take on a young partner who deserved to own at least some of the stable.

"Another mystery solved," Fred said happily.

Scooby grinned and picked a piece of hay from his teeth. "Rooby-rooby-roo!"

Camp Terranova was just terrific! That's what the kids from Mystery, Inc. were thinking as they sat on the front porch of the main lodge building. They'd signed on as counselors and this was their first night. All the campers were asleep and it was time to relax.

"What a great day this has been," Daphne said. "Tennis, hiking, swimming. This camp has everything."

Shaggy wiped his chocolate-coated hands on a white apron he wore over his clothing. He and Scooby were working in the mess hall, serving food to the campers. They also

30

helped in the kitchen. Being so close to food was like a dream come true for them. For one thing, they were allowed to eat all the leftover desserts. "This might just be the greatest job I've ever had," Shaggy said.

"Reah, ra rest rob re rever rad!" Scooby agreed as he slurped the last of his ice-cream soda.

"It might be the *only* job you two ever had," Velma quipped.

"Scoob and I have had jobs," Shaggy argued, looking hurt. "Solving mysteries is a job. It's work."

Fred stopped strumming his guitar. "That's sure true," he said. "But there won't be any mysteries to solve out here. Everything is peaceful and quiet."

"So you may think," said a deep voice from the doorway.

The gang turned and saw a man with wild, wiry white hair, a white beard, and dark glasses. He wore a baggy Hawaiian shirt and a black beret. "Don't you know that Mars, Venus, and Earth are perfectly aligned right now?"

31

"Well, as science counselor, I don't think that's exactly true," Velma objected.

"You're wrong!" the man snapped. "They *are* aligned! And when the planets line up, the last of the Von Wolftrap family makes the change."

"Like, why does he need to make change?" Shaggy asked. "Are there candy machines around here?"

"No! No!" the man shouted. "He doesn't *make* change! He changes! He changes into the Baron Von Wolftrap wolfman!"

Shaggy and Scooby jumped up. "Uh, uh, uh . . . wolfman?" Shaggy asked, turning pale.

"Yes," the man said. "No one sees him until . . ."

"Until what?" Shaggy asked in a shaky voice.

"Until the change, of course!" the man answered. "Then everyone hears from him — and *feels* his sharp teeth!"

Shaggy and Scooby looked at each other, then bolted down the path and out of sight. The man just laughed and left the porch.

32

A young woman came around the side of the lodge. It was Diana Gonzalez, the camp's owner. "That's Sid, our drama counselor. He's always kind of . . . dramatic. What was he telling you?" Diana sat down on the steps beside Velma.

"He was telling us about the Baron Von Wolftrap wolfman." Velma let out a chuckle. "Isn't that silly?"

"I'm afraid it's not," Diana said. "Last night I heard a strange howling in the woods. Frankly, I'm worried."

"Have you ever seen it?" Daphne asked.

"I did see something streaking through the woods once," Diana said.

"How long have you owned this camp?" Velma asked her.

"I won it on a game show when I was eighteen," Diana recalled. "Isn't that crazy? I went on the game show because I wanted to become an actress and I hoped someone might see me on TV. Instead I became a camp owner. I'd like to sell it, but so far I haven't found any buyers. Oh, well."

With a shrug, she got up and went up the

stairs. "Good night. Sleep tight." She went into the lodge, shutting the door behind her.

"How can we sleep tight after *that* story?" Daphne said. "Could it be true?"

"Oh, come on," Fred scoffed. "There are no such things as wolfmen. You know that."

"You're right," Daphne said. "Let's head back to our cabins and try to get some sleep. I wonder where Scooby and Shaggy went."

"Probably under their beds, shivering," Velma said with a laugh. Daphne and Fred laughed, too. Together they began walking down the dirt path heading to their cabins. But they stopped as an eerie sound filled the air.

"*Ow-ow-owoooooooooooooooooooooooooo!*"

"Baron Von Wolftrap wolfman?" Daphne asked slowly.

"Of course not," Fred said.

The gang took several steps forward — then they heard it again. "*Ow-ow-ow-oooooooooooooooooo!*"

"It's probably just a coyote or something in the woods," Daphne said, sounding nervous. The gang continued up the path, but they moved a little more quickly.

As they neared their cabins, they saw Scooby and Shaggy streak by them, running at top speed. "Scooby! Shaggy! Where are you going?"

"Ask him!" Shaggy shouted back.

"Jinkies!" Velma cried when she saw what was chasing Scooby and Shaggy. It was a creature — eight feet tall, covered in hair, with white, shining fangs and razor-sharp claws.

"Baron Von Wolftrap wolfman!" Fred shouted.

The wolfman heard his name and stopped. He stared at Fred and growled. Then he stomped forward, heading right toward Fred, Velma, and Daphne.

The kids stood stock-still, staring, frozen with fear. Then they whirled around and began to run.

"I thought there were no such things as wolfmen!" Daphne reminded Fred as she ran alongside him.

"There aren't," he replied.

"Then why are we running?" Velma asked.

"Do you have a better idea?" Fred returned.

Velma didn't, so she kept running with Fred and Daphne. They ran up to the lodge porch and peered out into the night. The wolfman was gone.

"We'd better check on the campers," Daphne said. They headed back out to check each of the cabins.

The kids were sleeping soundly, all but one. "Look over there," Daphne said. On one cot a camper had dug completely under the blankets. The child was shaking so fiercely that the covers moved. "Poor kid," Daphne said.

Fred, Velma, and Daphne tiptoed over to the terrified camper and gently drew back the blanket. But it was no camper — it was Shaggy and Scooby! They were huddled together, quaking in fear.

"Shaggy! Scooby!" Velma whispered sharply. "Get up!"

Still shaking, Shaggy and Scooby slid out of bed. "Like, it's been great being a counselor. I'm ready to go. So long," said Shaggy.

"Forget it," Fred said. "We have to stay up and make sure the kids are safe."

The gang didn't get much sleep that night. In the morning they were tired, but after breakfast Fred, Velma, and Daphne were ready to go on the hike they'd promised the campers. Many of the campers had heard wolf sounds during the night and all the kids were talking about it.

Scooby and Shaggy had to stay in the kitchen to prepare for lunch. "I always feel braver around food," Shaggy said, hugging a watermelon.

Willie, the tennis counselor, bounded by in his white shorts and shirt as Fred, Daphne, and Velma were heading into the woods. "Have you seen Diana?" he asked.

"No," Fred said.

Willie's shoulders slumped. "She's always so busy with this camp. I'm wealthy. If she'd marry me she wouldn't need to work. I wish she'd just close this place down."

Fred, Velma, and Daphne exchanged suspicious looks. Was he serious? How far would he go to shut down the camp?

As they walked through the woods, Velma felt something crunch under her feet. Looking down, she saw a pair of dark sunglasses. She picked up the glasses and slipped them into her skirt pocket.

After the hike, Fred, Velma, and Daphne brought the campers back to the lodge for lunch. Shaggy and Scooby were waiting for them. "The fish came wrapped in some newspaper," Shaggy said, "and as I was unwrapping it I saw this newspaper article."

He handed the scrap of paper to Fred. The gang gathered around to read it. It was about a famous director and the new horror movie he would be directing. Fred looked at his friends. "I think it's time to set a trap."

"Come on, Scoob! Would you do it for a Scooby Snack?" Daphne coaxed. She held out the box of Scooby Snacks.

"Roh, rall right," Scooby gave in. He dug into the box.

Fred came into the cabin holding a wolf costume for Scooby to put on. "After all, Scooby," he said as he helped Scooby step into it, "all dogs are descended from wolves. You're a natural for the part of Count Von Wolf-Scooby."

After cleaning up the supper dishes, Shaggy came into the cabin. "Zoinks!" he cried when he saw Scooby dressed like a werewolf. "You look like the real thing, Scoob!"

"Let's hope Baron Von Wolftrap thinks so," Velma said. "Come on. Everyone else is over at the campfire. This is the perfect time for us to nab the wolfman."

Beside one of the cabins, Daphne sat on a flat boulder and pretended to read a book. Scooby hid in a bush, while Fred, Velma, and Shaggy took their places.

It didn't take long before they heard the crunch of footsteps in the forest. "*Ow-ow-owooooooooooooooo!*" Baron Von Wolftrap wolfman sprang at Daphne.

At just the same moment, Scooby leaped out of the bushes with his arms stretched wide. He growled ferociously at the wolfman.

"Ahhhhhh!" the wolfman screamed. He turned to run into the woods when Fred and Shaggy shone two bright lanterns into his eyes. He staggered back, allowing Shaggy to throw a large white sheet over his head.

Fred and Velma helped Shaggy hold on to the struggling figure beneath the blanket. "When I take this blanket off we'll know if we were right about who Baron Von Wolftrap wolfman really is!" Fred shouted.

Do you think you know who it is? See the next page to find out if you're right!

"Just as we thought!" Fred said. "Sid, the drama counselor. You're really Sid Snookerman, the famous movie director. Now that we see you without those dark glasses and that fake beard, we'd know you anywhere."

Sid Snookerman pulled off the high shoes that made him appear eight feet tall. "Well, at least I don't have to wear these anymore," he said.

The gang had narrowed their suspects down to three. Diana Gonzalez wanted to sell her camp. She might have thought that having a werewolf at her camp would attract attention. But it might have backfired and frightened people out of buying the camp.

Willie, the tennis counselor, wanted Diana to shut down the camp and he might have wanted to scare campers away. But he loved Diana and wouldn't want to hurt her.

When Velma found dark glasses in the forest, she suspected Sid. Then Shaggy found the article about the horror film. The famous director was Sid Snookerman. The gang recognized Sid from his picture. When they read that the movie was about a werewolf, they realized what was going on. It was all a publicity stunt to create interest in his new movie. If everyone was talking about a werewolf that was loose in the woods, they'd be anxious to see the wolfman movie.

In the end, Sid apologized. He bought the camp from Diana so he could film his movie there. She married Willie and went off to Hollywood to become an actress.

Fred, Velma, and Daphne all won small parts in the movie, while Scooby and Shaggy continued to work in the kitchen feeding the actors and crew of the werewolf movie. They had fun and ate quite a lot that summer.

Or, as Scooby put it: "Rooby-rooby-(burp!)-roo!"

"Come on, Scooby, Shaggy! You're not afraid of the roller coaster, are you?" Velma called. She was standing in line for the roller-coaster ride at the Goofy Island Amusement Park. Fred and Daphne were there, too.

Scooby and Shaggy had their faces buried in giant pink clouds of cotton candy. "Shmignitwrogpuf," Shaggy seemed to say.

"Rhmigrofgruruf," Scooby added.

"What did they say?" Daphne asked Velma.

"We said, like, we're busy," Shaggy said as he picked his head up out of the cotton candy.

43

"Re're rizzy," Scooby agreed.

"Let's go on without them," Fred suggested. "We owe it to Mr. Filch to find out who's been tampering with his rides. Maybe we'll find a clue on the roller coaster."

Philip Filch was a man who had contacted the gang's detective agency, Mystery, Inc., to solve a case for him. He'd said someone was tampering with his amusement park rides and scaring away his customers.

The previous ride came to a stop and the passengers got off. "Everything seems okay," Daphne observed.

Fred, Daphne, and Velma got into their shared seat — the very first car — and closed the safety bar. The car began moving slowly up the track. It reached a high peak, then stalled.

When the kids looked back to see what was going on, they realized that their car was the only one at the top. All the other riders were still sitting below, waiting to start.

"I have a bad feeling about this," Fred said.

"Uh-huh." Daphne and Velma nodded.

The next thing they knew, they were speeding down the slope faster than they had ever gone on a roller coaster. Fred, Daphne, and Velma clung to the safety bar. They swept around a corner, which whipped their heads sharply to the right, and saw that their worst fears might come true.

"Jinkies!" Velma shouted. The track ahead of them had been bent outward at the highest spot. If the car went over that bend, it would go sailing out into the ocean.

Daphne screamed. Fred covered his face. Velma took off her glasses — she didn't want to see what was coming next!

Just as the car was about to go over, it suddenly slammed to a halt. The three riders looked at the beach and let out a long sigh of relief.

The car backed up and slowly returned them to the starting point. The ride attendant hurried up to them. "Are you all right?" he asked anxiously. "I don't know what happened. The button jammed. And someone must have unhooked your car. I don't know why these things keep happening."

Velma smoothed her hair and put her glasses back on. "What other things have happened?" she asked as calmly as she could.

"Terrible things," he told her. "The loop-de-loop wouldn't stop looping for an hour yesterday. The Ferris wheel went one hundred miles per hour. No one could find their way out of the fun house because the doors were all locked from the outside. And someone put glue in Bingo the Clown's extra-large shoes."

Mr. Filch ran up the path to see them. He was a short, fat man who wore a baseball cap. "I saw what happened. Are you kids okay? This is so dreadful!" he fretted.

Before they could answer, a man in coveralls approached Mr. Filch. "I need your signature on this work order to fix the Ferris wheel," he requested, handing a paper to Mr. Filch.

Daphne was next to him and watched as he wrote his name. She noticed he had an odd way of forming the initial *F*. It looked to her as though he'd written Mr. Zilch instead of Mr. Filch.

"Is there anyone you suspect of doing these things?" Fred asked him.

"Yes," he replied. "I suspect my ex-girlfriend Mamie Mason. She works over at the basketball game. She's got a real grudge against me."

The three friends walked through the park to a long stretch that featured nothing but games. They found Scooby and Shaggy using a machine where they had to lift out stuffed animals with a handheld crane.

Shaggy was very good at this game. He had built up a three-foot pile of stuffed animals.

"Wow, Shaggy, you've almost emptied the machine," Daphne said, gazing inside.

"Thanks," Shaggy replied. "I wish I could find one of these filled with boxes of Scooby Snacks."

"Wait a minute," Daphne said, still peering into the machine. "There's something strange down there. Try to grab it, Shaggy."

Shaggy got a hold of it and pulled it up.

"It's a rubber mask," Fred said when Shaggy pulled it out of the machine. He held it up so they could all examine it.

"It's so real looking," Daphne commented.

"This face looks familiar," Velma added. "But I don't know where I've seen him before."

"Let's go talk to Mamie Mason," Fred suggested.

They walked down the lane until they found a woman in her fifties with frizzy blond hair. "Play the basketball game. Four balls for a dollar. Everybody's a winner!" she shouted at the passing crowd.

The gang asked her about Mr. Filch. "He's right. I hate him. He left me standing at the altar on our wedding day, claimed he just changed his mind — the rat!"

Daphne held up the mask. "Do you know anyone who looks like this mask?"

Mamie studied it for several minutes. "He looks awfully familiar. Maybe he was an old customer of mine or something. Yeah. He might have been."

"Now where have Scooby and Shaggy gone to?" Velma asked, looking around. The two friends had disappeared again.

"Over there," Fred said. Shaggy and Scooby had found a photo booth and were putting on old-fashioned costumes to have their pictures taken. Shaggy was dressed like a cowboy. Scooby wore a horse outfit. The gang went over to watch.

As the photographer fussed with Shaggy's cowboy hat, Daphne glanced at the far wall of the booth, where photos of previous customers hung. Her eyes widened as she looked at one of them. It was a man dressed in a top hat. He'd autographed his own picture — Zacko Zane.

Daphne held the mask up to the picture to compare. "Hey, guys, come here. Look at this. It's him."

"It sure is," Fred agreed. They discussed the case a few more minutes, then Fred folded his arms. "If you're thinking what I'm thinking," he said to them, "it's time to set a trap."

"Try two Scooby Snacks," Velma whispered to Daphne.

Daphne nodded and took two Scooby Snacks from the box. "Come on, Scooby, will you do it for two Scooby Snacks?"

Scooby shook his head.

"Two Scooby Snacks each and an ice-cream sundae," Shaggy said. "That's our final offer."

"Deal," Daphne agreed.

Fred slipped the rubber mask of Zacko Zane over Scooby's head. Then Scooby climbed up on Shaggy's shoulders while Daphne and Velma wrapped a long overcoat around the two of them. Fred quickly buttoned it from top to bottom.

They walked to the back of the fun house and let Scooby and Shaggy in the back door. "You don't have to do anything," Fred told them. "Just stand here. We'll do the rest."

Daphne walked up to the front of the fun

house with Mr. Filch. "We want to look for clues inside," she told him. "But we need you to stand guard outside to make sure nothing unusual happens."

"Oh, yes, sure," he agreed.

Daphne, Velma, and Fred went into the fun house and waited a few minutes. Then Daphne ran out and grabbed Mr. Filch's hand. "You have to come in!" she said. "We've found something really horrible. You have to see it."

Mr. Filch frowned. "Oh, all right," he said as he followed Daphne into the fun house.

"It's all the way at the very back of the house," Daphne said, leading him through the dark corners, distorted mirrors, and confusing turns. "It's right here."

The moment he turned the corner and saw Scooby and Shaggy disguised as the towering figure of Zacko Zane, Mr. Filch turned to run. But he couldn't figure out where the real exit was. And the mirrors reflected more and more Zacko Zanes at him.

Finally, Mr. Filch bounced off one of the

mirrors and fell to the floor. Velma and Fred stepped out of their hiding places behind the wall.

Fred grabbed the man's ears. Just as he'd suspected, they felt rubbery. "You're not the real Philip Filch. When I take off this mask we'll see who you really are!"

Do you know who's under the mask? See the next page to find out if you're right!

"**E**xactly as you figured, Daphne," Fred said. "It's Zacko Zane." The man looked the same as the picture and the mask, only his nose was crooked and he had a long nasty scar running diagonally from his forehead to his chin.

"Philip Filch did this to me!" he cried. "His Ferris wheel was unsafe, so I deserve my revenge."

"I remember now! I read about you in the newspaper. You stood up on the Ferris wheel and rocked it," Velma said. "Everyone screamed at you to sit down. They even stopped the Ferris wheel. But you kept rocking it until you fell."

"So? I was just having fun," Zacko Zane defended himself lamely. "It was still Filch's fault. He made me so ugly that I had to make a mask to cover my face."

As Scooby climbed down from Shaggy's shoulders, Shaggy pulled the mask off him. "You must mean this mask," he said, holding it up.

"Hey, where'd you get that?" Zacko Zane

demanded. "When I changed that mask for this one, I stashed it where no one would ever find it."

Shaggy grinned proudly. "Like, you didn't count on the King of the Crane Machine coming around."

How did the gang figure out that Philip Filch was really Zacko Zane? Daphne's first clue was the *Z*. It changed Mr. Filch's name to Mr. Zilch. Zilch is a slang way of saying "nothing." Daphne suspected that this might be a little private joke the man was playing to amuse himself. Seeing the *Z* also made her recognize it later on Zacko Zane's autographed picture. The two *Z*s matched.

The only other suspects were the roller-coaster attendant and Mamie Mason. The attendant had the ability to rig the rides, but he had no motive. Mamie Mason had a reason to be mad and want revenge on Philip Filch, but she had an alibi — she had to run her game booth.

"Where is the real Philip Filch?" Daphne asked.

Fred had slipped out quietly and returned

with a worn and tired man. "I found him in a closet right over here," he said.

"I called you kids to come investigate because of all the strange things happening," the man explained.

"And then the fake Mr. Filch had to play along so we wouldn't suspect him," Velma finished.

In the end, Zacko Zane went to jail. Philip Filch explained to Mamie that he hadn't come to their wedding because he was locked in a closet. (It had been Zacko Zane disguised as Philip who said he'd changed his mind.) And Filch offered Scooby and Shaggy all the cotton candy they could eat.

"Look at these colorful fish," Daphne said, gazing through the floor of the glass-bottom boat. A school of orange-and-white-striped fish swam below, their graceful fins shining in the clear Caribbean water.

"That reminds me, Goldfish crackers would be nice for lunch," Shaggy said, licking his lips.

"You just had breakfast!" Velma protested.

"You're right," Shaggy agreed. "I should have a sandwich for an after-breakfast snack. I'll never make it all the way to lunch without a little something."

"Reah, a rafter-reakfast rack!" Scooby said, also licking his lips.

Fred laughed. "You guys are too much. Here we are on a beautiful tropical island, about to scuba dive around an ancient shipwreck, and all you can think about is eating!"

The captain of the boat, Fishy Wales, turned toward the gang. "Soon you will see some of the most amazing sights of your life. This boat went down in the 1930s during a storm. Coral beds have grown around it. Many octopuses have also made homes within it."

"Are we the only ones diving today?" Daphne asked him.

Captain Wales nodded. "Business has been very bad. You are the only trip we have taken out for the last month. People have become afraid of the shipwreck. That is why my boss invited Mystery, Inc. to investigate."

Captain Wales let out his anchor. The gang pulled on their wet suits, air tanks, flippers, and masks. Even Scooby had an outfit that he put on.

57

"Hey, guys," Shaggy said, laughing. "Look at Scooby — he's Scuba-dooba-doo."

Scooby sucked in his cheeks to make a fish face and pretended to swim underwater.

One by one, the gang stepped off the boat and plunged into the water. They'd taken lessons before coming to the island but this was their first dive without an instructor, and they were all feeling a little nervous. They swam among the barnacle-covered metal beams of the sunken boat. Shy octopuses swam away as they approached.

Sunlight filtered through the crystal-blue water, but as they turned corners into the hallways and rooms of the sunken ship, it grew shadowy and more difficult to see.

Fred swam into a large room that might have once been a ballroom. It had long, elegantly curved openings where windows once were. And there was a platform that could have been a stage.

Fred felt his way along the far wall of the room. His hand slipped into a hole in the wall. He peered into the hole and saw his own masked face looking back at him. It startled him, and he recoiled. *It must just be a reflection from my mask*, he decided.

The others swam in to join Fred. Daphne spotted something glistening on the floor and reached down for it. It was a coin, and Daphne hoped it might be old and valuable. She stuck it into the small pocket on her diving belt.

Suddenly the stage area began glowing with a mysterious white light. The gang held on to one another, not knowing what to expect. Then music filled the room. It was old-fashioned swing music from the 1930s.

In the glowing light, couples appeared on the dance floor. The men wore suits and the ladies had fancy beaded dresses. They swirled in time to the music.

Then the dancing people faded and a skeleton appeared. Its gray hair floated in the water, and its dress was torn and rotted. It spread its bony arms and rose in the water.

The gang turned and swam out of the room as fast as they could. As they zoomed down a hallway, a gate dropped in front of them, blocking their path. When they turned, the skeleton was right behind them. The kids turned down a hall to the right and found their way out of the wreck.

They'd learned that it's not safe to swim quickly up to the surface when scuba diving. But they went up as fast as possible. Captain Wales helped each of them into the boat.

"We can tell your boss, like, why he has no business," Shaggy said as he pulled off his scuba mask. "That's one haunted shipwreck down there."

Captain Wales nodded. "I thought so. It serves my boss, Mr. Waverly, right. I told him not to do business here. This is an underwater graveyard. People shouldn't be diving here."

"We'd better go have a talk with him," Velma suggested.

Back at the dock, the gang disembarked, glad to be back onshore. Captain Wales saw his nephew walking toward him and waved. His nephew was about twenty and wore headphones connected to a DVD player. As he listened to music with one ear, he spoke on his cell phone, listening with his other ear. "Got to go," he said to the person on the other end. "Just press the RECORD button like I told you and see if it works. Bye."

He smiled at the gang and stuck out his hand to shake. "I'm Wiley Wales," he said. "Pleased to meet you."

"Wiley has his own TV cable company," Captain Wales said proudly. "He is very good with everything electronic."

Wiley smiled at his uncle. "Uncle Fishy practically raised me after my father passed away," he said fondly. He asked his uncle, "Can I borrow the boat tonight, around nine? I want to take some friends out for a spin."

"Sure thing," his uncle agreed. "Mr. Waverly says I can use it anytime after six o'clock."

The gang said good-bye to them and walked up the dock to the office of Mr. Waverly, owner of Waverly Waves Scuba Tours. They found the man sitting behind his desk and told him what they'd seen.

"Not that story again!" he shouted angrily. "Fishy Wales has been telling me that place is haunted for years. I'm sick of hearing it. You know, I'm so sick of hearing that story that I'd like to fire him. I can't, though. I'd have to prove to the island employment board that he's a bad worker. But he's a great worker!"

"Then why would you want to fire him?" Velma asked.

"He annoys me with those ghost stories. Maybe if business gets bad enough I can fire him. Then when business picks up again, I'll hire someone else to run my tour. But for now, I'll fire you. Mystery, Inc., you're fired!"

The gang walked out of the office. "Gee, we've never been fired before," Daphne said.

"Oh, who cares?" Velma replied. "I want to solve this case, anyway."

"Okay," Fred agreed. "Daphne and I will snoop around the outside of the office. Velma, you check out the boat again. Shaggy and Scooby, you look around the dock."

"Like, yay," Shaggy said. "There might be a food stand on the dock."

"Reah, rood rand," Scooby agreed happily.

Velma went down to the boat. It was empty. Captain Wales wasn't around. She didn't find anything until she came to a round black carrying case. It was soaking wet, but the DVD inside was dry.

When she met her friends again, she showed them the case and the DVD inside. The words *Version 1* were written on it in permanent marker.

"I think we can crack this case right here and now," Fred said. "This is my plan. . . ."

Do you think you know who's behind the mystery of the haunted shipwreck? Turn the page to find out if you're right!

Wiley Wales was responsible for the whole thing. Here's how Fred, Velma, Daphne, Scooby, and Shaggy got him to admit it.

Around nine o'clock, the gang was set up and sitting together in a rowboat at the end of the dock. They couldn't be seen from the dock, and that was just how they wanted it. After a few minutes, Wiley Wales showed up with five of his friends.

"Now!" Fred whispered to the gang.

A horrible bony skeleton suddenly appeared at the end of the dock. Its hair floated around its white, eyeless skull.

Velma peered over the dock and watched Wiley's friends race away back up the dock. Wiley stood there, wide-eyed and frozen with terror.

Daphne sat forward in the boat. "Wiley! Wiley!" she sang out. "I'm coming to get you. You have insulted my memory."

"But you're just fake!" Wiley said in a shaky voice. "I made you out of a plastic skeleton and a wig."

That was all the gang needed to hear.

Fred instantly shut off the film he was playing on the wide-screen TV he'd set up on the end of the dock. He and the gang climbed up on the dock and confronted him.

"We knew you set up the whole haunted shipwreck," Velma said.

"When I saw myself in that hole in the room, I didn't realize at first that I was looking into a projector lens," Fred said. "But later I figured it out. You played a DVD on some kind of screen at the back of the room, didn't you?"

Wiley nodded, looking ashamed. "It's true."

"When I looked at the coin I picked up today I saw that it was dated from this year," Daphne said. "It was shiny and new. Your uncle said no one had been down there for a month, so it told me someone had been in that room recently — someone your uncle hadn't taken there."

"Didn't you recognize your own work when we played version one of your ghostly production just now?" Velma asked.

"I should have, but I made it so long ago

65

I'd forgotten about it," he admitted. "Version two is much better, don't you think?"

"Yes, it is," Fred agreed.

The gang had suspected that Mr. Waverly was trying to ruin his own business just to get rid of Fishy Wales. Then when they found the DVD in Fishy Wales's boat, they thought he might be a suspect. But he had no reason to try to haunt the ship. Wiley Wales had the technical know-how to pull this off, but they couldn't figure out his motive. They soon learned it.

"Why did you try to scare us?" Daphne asked.

Wiley sighed, then began to speak. "My uncle is a great guy, but he believes in ghosts. He hates going to that wreck because he believes it's haunted. Most of the people around here believe that. The story has gotten around, even to the tourists. That's why business has fallen off."

"That makes sense," Fred commented.

"Then I heard Mr. Waverly had hired Mystery, Inc. I figured if I could get you guys to tell Waverly that the place really was haunted, he would move his dive site some-where else and Uncle Fishy would feel bet-ter. I worked with some guys I know who make underwater equipment."

"Well, we have to admit your motives were good," Daphne said.

"And you did a great job haunting the place," Velma agreed.

In the end, Mr. Waverly did move his dive site, the customers came back, and Fishy Wales was much happier.

Shaggy and Scooby were also much hap-pier that night when the gang went to the All-You-Can-Eat Fisherman's Restaurant. Scooby and Shaggy broke the all-time all-you-can-eat record.

"Rooby-rooby-roo!" Scooby shouted.

"Like, what was the rush?" Shaggy asked as Fred pulled the Mystery Machine into an empty parking lot behind the public library.

"Something upset my aunt Dolores enough for her to call and ask for our help," Velma replied, climbing out of the van.

"The library is usually busy, especially in the summer," Daphne said, looking around for signs of activity — and finding none.

Fred held the library door open for the gang to file through. "Don't they have the summer reading club anymore?" he asked.

68

Shaggy stopped in front of a big poster. "This says they do." He pointed. "And, Scooby, there's a big party next week for everyone who reads at least five books. They're having food. We could do that."

Scooby stared at the pictures of cookies and cake on the poster. "Ruh-huh!"

"Which reminds me" — Shaggy turned to his friends — "we didn't have time to pack a snack and I'm . . ." Shaggy's stomach rumbled loudly.

"Shh!" Velma put her finger over her lips. "This is supposed to be a quiet place, remember?" she whispered.

Scooby's stomach echoed Shaggy's rumblings. "Ruh-roh!" Scooby said.

A thin woman with graying hair pulled into a severe bun frowned at them. Shaggy turned back to the poster.

"Let's see if we can find Aunt Dolores," Velma said quietly.

As Shaggy turned away from the summer reading poster, he knocked into a young woman walking toward the door. She was carrying a stack of old books.

"Like, sorry," he apologized as the woman chased after a small silver disk rolling across the floor. Velma stopped the disk with the toe of her shoe, then picked it up and examined it before handing it to the woman. It was dusty, so Velma wiped her hands on her skirt before putting them in her pockets.

"Bonnie, dear, is that my hole punch?" the desk librarian asked. "I thought you were going to bring it right back — what — several weeks ago?"

"Yes, ma'am, I'm sorry. I must have stuck it in my pocket, and I didn't find it until I put on these pants again. I'm sorry," she apologized again. Bonnie quickly returned the hole punch to the desk while Fred and Daphne gathered the books she'd dropped.

"Thanks," Bonnie said in a soft voice, holding out her arms to take them.

"Do you think we could keep a couple of these, or are you checking them out?" Daphne asked.

The woman hesitated a moment. "Of course you may. But you'll want to be careful. These are rare copies of old cookbooks. I'm doing an evaluation for the library and brought these out to look at them more closely. Do you like to cook?" she asked Daphne.

"Not as much as Shaggy and Scooby like to eat. I thought these might keep them occupied until we can find some real food." Daphne opened a cookbook to a picture spread and held it up for Scooby and Shaggy to see.

The woman sitting behind the desk cleared her throat loudly and glared at the gang.

"Velma!" A short woman emerged from the back of the room and grabbed Velma, kissing her on both cheeks, then hugging her tightly.

"Hi, Aunt Dolores." Velma returned her aunt's hug.

"I'm so glad you could come," Aunt Dolores continued. She made no attempt to speak quietly. "You can see we have a big problem — no customers!" She swept her arm around the room, which seemed huge and empty. The only people there were Aunt Dolores; the members of Mystery, Inc.; the frowning librarian, Bonnie, and a red-haired boy, whose face was hidden by a book with a picture of a monster on the cover.

"We thought it seemed quiet," Fred said.

"And it shouldn't be," Aunt Dolores continued. "The room should be buzzing, dancing, alive with children discovering the joy of reading."

"Silent reading," said the prim librarian behind the checkout desk. "I have to say that this noise level is more the way a library should be. All those noisy, sticky children tearing books off shelves, leaving them any old place." She shook her head as she toyed with the nameplate on her desk identifying her as "Miss Joan."

"I remember you," Daphne said. "You were the librarian when we were in the summer reading club."

"And back then, it was reading that we focused on — not all this singing, dancing, and discussing that all the young librarians seem to think is so important." Miss Joan looked pointedly at Aunt Dolores. She turned to Velma. "You still hold the record for the most books read in one summer."

The boy at the table slammed the monster book shut and laid it on top of a pile of books towering beside him. "Not for long," he called across the room. "Not if Great Scott continues at his present pace."

The gang looked from the boy to Aunt Dolores for an explanation.

"Jack is determined to break Velma's record no matter what. In fact, even the Bookworm can't scare him away," Aunt Dolores said with a nervous laugh.

"Bookworm?" Shaggy gulped and held the cookbook away from his body. "A little tiny bookworm, I hope." He and Scooby moved closer to the rest of the gang.

"I'm afraid this Bookworm is large and hungry," Aunt Dolores said. "And it scared away all my summer readers except Jack — or Great Scott, as he prefers to be called."

"Good riddance," Miss Joan mumbled, straightening the papers on her desk.

"Then . . . then feed it," suggested Shaggy.

"It seems to like a steady diet of books, and we can't afford to let it continue to eat them," Aunt Dolores explained as she led the way to a large table at the back of the room. Everyone sat down around it while Aunt Dolores explained the mysterious events that had been occurring at the library that summer.

"We were in the swing of summer reading. I had a roomful of customers choosing books, checking out books, even staying behind to read their books, like they couldn't wait long enough to carry them home." Aunt Dolores looked happy at the thought of all that reading.

"So many of the books had been checked out of the main reading room, we opened the stacks where we store some of the older books that don't circulate much. I was working the desk when I heard screams coming out of the stacks, then several children ran out like they were being chased."

Scooby and Shaggy nervously looked over their shoulders toward the library stacks.

Then they moved their chairs closer to each other.

"What was back there?" Velma asked, leaning forward.

"All the children described seeing the same thing," Aunt Dolores said slowly. "A huge gray-and-white worm wriggling over the top of one of the bookshelves. It was Jack's sister, Jill, who was the first to call it the Bookworm."

"And did you go back there to see for yourself?" Fred asked.

Aunt Dolores nodded. "All we found were some crumbs of paper on the floor by the shelves where the Bookworm had been seen. And some of the books were completely gone, devoured by that hungry Bookworm."

"Has anyone seen this Bookworm since?" asked Velma.

"Yeah, you think it's still back there?" asked Shaggy, his voice cracking.

"Word spread quickly, and the only people who have had the nerve to go back to the stacks — even to come through the library doors — are Miss Joan and I, who work here, and Great Scott, who claims he's learned enough from all the books he's read this summer to know there's no such thing as a Bookworm. And Bonnie." Aunt Dolores paused a moment. "Bonnie used to work here until she opened a rare bookshop downtown. Business isn't good," she whispered, "so we're paying her to help us evaluate some of our older books to see if we have anything rare."

"Let's look around and see if we can find any clues," Velma suggested.

"Can't we eat something first?" asked Shaggy. "I don't know if I have the strength. . . ."

"No eating in the library!" Miss Joan said from her perch behind the desk.

"Yes, ma'am," said Shaggy meekly. Scooby scooted down in his chair.

"Let's have a chat with Jack and see if he can tell us anything else," Fred said. "Shaggy, you and Scooby go have a look in the stacks and see if you can find any clues."

"There's an entire section of cookbooks," Aunt Dolores said. "And maybe I can find something in the break room to tide you over until later," she whispered to Shaggy and Scooby with a wink. She pushed back from the table.

Slowly, Shaggy and Scooby headed toward the library stacks.

Fred, Velma, and Daphne approached the boy reading at the table near the door. "Hi, Jack," said Fred.

"I prefer to be called Great Scott," the boy replied, not bothering to lower his book.

"Have you seen the Bookworm?" asked Daphne.

Velma busied herself looking through the stack of titles sitting by Jack's elbow.

"No such thing," Jack said. "But if those other dorks want to believe it's real, better for me. My sister and I had a bet. The first one of us to break Velma's reading record doesn't have to do dishes for the rest of the summer. But now she's afraid to step inside the doors to check out a book. And, if you don't mind, I still have twenty books to read before I become the Great Scott of Summer Reading."

"I have to agree with Jack," Miss Joan said, motioning for Fred, Daphne, and Velma to join her at the desk. She lowered her voice. "It got rid of those pesky kids and left me and my books in lovely quiet."

Fred, Velma, and Daphne exchanged looks.

"Shall we join Shaggy and Scooby?" Velma asked. "I hope they aren't hungry enough to try to eat the food right out of the pages of those books," she said.

Daphne giggled, then clapped her hands over her mouth to stifle the sound. She didn't want to disrupt Miss Joan's quiet.

Shaggy and Scooby sat on the floor by the cookbooks, cookie crumbs hanging off their chins. "Your aunt was here," Shaggy said, "and she brought us the best cookies."

"Rum, rum," said Scooby.

Velma knelt on the floor nearby. She reached into her pocket, looked down at her fingers, then back to the floor. She paged through the book Shaggy had been reading and found a page with a hole in it. Velma took another book off the shelf and found an identical hole. "I think I know —"

A slithering sound interrupted Velma before she could finish her thought.

"Is that . . . ?" Shaggy leaped to his feet. Scooby leaped into his arms.

A gray-and-white head appeared over the top shelf of the bookcase.

"Zoinks! Let's get out of here!" Shaggy yelled.

Velma rose slowly to her feet and crossed her arms. "Not to worry. That's not the Bookworm, it's . . ."

Do you think you know who the Bookworm really is? Turn the page to see if you're right!

Velma reached up and pulled the mask off the bookworm's head.

"Bonnie!" cried Aunt Dolores, who'd run up to join the kids when she'd heard Shaggy yell.

"That's right," Velma said.

"At first we suspected Miss Joan, who seemed to enjoy the library's quiet since the Bookworm struck," Fred said.

"And Great Scott seemed willing to do anything to win the book contest this summer — even if he had to scare away all the competition!" Daphne declared.

"But we realized that Bonnie was the real culprit after I picked up the little silver cylinder she dropped when she bumped into Shaggy," Velma explained. "I had some dots of paper stuck to my fingertips. I didn't want to litter in the library so I rubbed them off in my pocket until I could find a wastebasket. And when I came back to the stacks, I saw that the same dots, or 'crumbs,' littered the floor where the Bookworm had 'lunched.'

"As soon as I saw those dots," Velma continued, "I realized Bonnie wasn't carrying those books out to get a better look at them. She was stealing rare books out of the library stacks to sell in her store! She used a hole punch to mark those she had already looked at and discarded as worthless."

"So Bonnie created the Bookworm to scare off the customers who were slowing down her theft of valuable books from the library," Fred said.

"That's right," Daphne put in. "And also so that all the library's customers would be forced to shop at her store!"

"Bonnie, is all this true?" Aunt Dolores asked.

"Yes," admitted Bonnie, hanging her head. She looked very ashamed. "I'm so sorry! I didn't know what to do. I wanted you to be proud of me when I opened my store, but I just couldn't get any business and I didn't want to disappoint you."

"Oh, Bonnie, you should never have worried about that!" Aunt Dolores said kindly. "You can always come back to your old job at the library."

"Really?" Bonnie said, her sad face brightening.

"Of course," said Aunt Dolores, hugging the girl. Then she turned to the gang. "How can I ever thank you for helping us?"

"I can think of a way," Velma said, grinning. "Just invite us to your summer reading party next week."

"Reah! Reah!" said Scooby.

Aunt Dolores laughed. "Of course you're invited! It wouldn't be a party without you."

"Rooby-rooby-roo!" cheered Scooby.

Fred, Velma, Daphne, Shaggy, and Scooby peered through the windshield of the Mystery Machine at the lighthouse looming ahead of them. It looked as if it were rising out of the ocean. All around it, spread over the beach, were lumber and construction equipment.

"This is the hot new music club Rich Davies told us about?" Daphne asked.

"Not quite," Fred said. "This is where Rich wants to build a new club, but he can't get anyone to work on the renovations. That's why we're here."

83

"Like, *we're* going to fix up this place?" Shaggy asked.

"I don't think so, Shaggy. Rich is going to meet us here to tell us what the mystery is." Fred looked in the rearview mirror. "Here he comes now."

A vintage red Mustang convertible pulled up beside the van. The handsome young man behind the wheel beeped his car horn three times, then hopped out of the car without opening the door. He tapped his toe impatiently while the gang climbed out of the Mystery Machine.

"What do you think?" he asked, directing his question to Fred. "Great site for a club, isn't it? Picture a covered dance floor, colored lights flashing, live music, food and drink inside. . . ."

Shaggy and Scooby perked up at the mention of food. "What kind of food?" Shaggy interrupted. "You got any samples?"

Rich shook his head. "I'm thinking drinks, appetizers, maybe burgers and dogs. I guess there's no sense in finalizing the menu until there's a kitchen," he said.

"It's cool, Rich," Fred answered. "Does the light work?" He pointed at the tower atop the lighthouse.

"Not yet, but it will. I swear it will. As soon as we get rid of the pirate." Rich Davies paused. "You see, that's the problem."

"A pirate? There have been too many pirates in my life already. No thank you, sir. You with me on this one, Scooby?" Shaggy headed back across the sand to the Mystery Machine. Scooby was right behind him.

"Don't mind them. Tell us more about your pirate," Fred urged the club owner.

"He's a musical guy, I'll give him that, but he's scaring away all the workers. Every morning when they arrive, the same thing happens. First, there's a heavy backbeat — *ga, chunka, ga, chunka, ga, ga, ga, dewp, dewp, dewp, dewp, bum, bum, bum.* Then a guitar joins in with a screaming hot lick that ends in a high, piercing screech. Finally, the pirate appears on the roof of the lighthouse. He's got a full black beard hiding his face, skull and crossbones on his hat, and he starts growling and waving a big sword. He's

85

one scary dude!" Rich reached into the Mustang and pulled out a tape player. "I set this up and recorded the music one morning." He hit the PLAY button, and music with a heavy bass beat blared out of the tape deck.

Velma covered her ears, and Rich turned down the volume. He glanced up at the roof of the lighthouse as if the music might summon the pirate, but nothing happened.

"Has he threatened anyone? Hurt anyone?" Daphne asked.

"No one's stayed around long enough to give him a chance," Rich replied, clicking off the tape player.

"Are there any stories of pirates or pirate treasure connected to this lighthouse?" asked Velma.

"Not that I know of. Are those guys going to come out of the van?" Rich asked, looking at Shaggy and Scooby peeking out the window of the Mystery Machine.

"Maybe when they get hungry," Velma said with a laugh.

A black pickup truck roared across the sand, music blasting. When the driver slammed on the brakes a few feet from the Mystery Machine, the truck fishtailed and the tires threw off a wave of sand.

The gang coughed and wiped sand from their eyes.

"What do you think you're doing?" Daphne sputtered.

The driver's door opened.

"Just trying to get your attention, beautiful." A tall, dark-haired boy climbed out. He was wearing jeans and a T-shirt with the words MIKE AND THE MOTORMOUTHS printed across the front. The Os looked like large open mouths ringed with red lips. "What's up, bro?" he asked Rich, lifting his hand for a high five.

"What are you doing out here?" Rich asked, frowning. He turned to the gang. "This is my brother, Mike — the musician."

"Dropped by to see if the club's happening yet," Mike said, looking toward the lighthouse. "Man, I'm getting tired of waiting for that big break you promised me. When's it going to happen?"

"As soon as this place is ready," Rich said.

"Mikey! Are you done yet?" a voice came from the pickup truck. A girl with striped blue, yellow, and red hair leaned out the window. Even from a distance, it was obvious she was chewing gum.

"I'm taking care of business here, woman," Mike yelled back at her. "Get out of the truck and join us." He turned back to the group and said, "That's my girl, Cheri. She has a band of her own, Cheri and the Pits."

"Interesting," said Daphne.

"Have you ever seen the pirate haunting your brother's lighthouse?" Fred asked Mike.

"I was the first one to ever see him. Rich sent me out here one morning to check on something for him and the next thing I knew, a pirate was looking down at me, waving a big old sword." Mike shook his head and glanced quickly up to the roof and away. "I haven't been very anxious to come back since then."

"Could we take a look around?" Velma asked Rich.

"Not a problem. Let me get the key."

Daphne walked to the truck. Cheri was humming a song and keeping time on the dashboard. "Hi, Cheri," she said. "Sounds like a great song. It's got a good beat."

"Do I know you?" Cheri asked, growing quiet.

"No, we're here to help Mike's brother. Mike was telling us about your band."

Cheri looked at Daphne from underneath her rainbow bangs. "What did he tell you? That we stink?"

"Not at all. He only mentioned that the two of you are in bands. Have you played many gigs?" Daphne asked.

Cheri shrugged. "A few. We're good. Better than the Motormouths, if you want to know the truth." She glanced nervously over her shoulder toward Mike. "And we'll prove it in time. But for now, Mike and I have decided that our music is our own business. I don't listen to his, and he doesn't listen to mine. It works out better that way. I don't want to be contaminated by the slop he writes, any-way." Cheri stuck her nose in the air.

89

"Why don't you come look around the lighthouse with us?" Daphne asked.

Cheri shook her head. "That place gives me the creeps. I'm headed for the beach — with or without him." She climbed out of the truck, grabbed a black tote bag, and headed toward the water. After a few steps, she stopped and turned back to Daphne. "Want to come with?" Cheri asked.

"Not today," Daphne answered. "I think I'll see what's up in the lighthouse."

Cheri shrugged, then turned and walked swiftly away.

As Daphne joined Fred and Rich by the lighthouse, Mike approached her. "What'd you do to my girlfriend to make her go away?" he asked.

"She said she wanted to go to the beach," Daphne said.

"If she'd spend more time on her music and less time on her suntan, she'd go a lot further. Morning, noon, and night, beach, beach, beach," Mike complained.

In the meantime, Velma had coaxed Shaggy and Scooby out of the van. As they headed toward the lighthouse, a loud voice stopped them in their tracks.

"Hey, you! What do you think you're doing? No dogs allowed on the beach," a voice called.

"Rho, re?" Scooby pointed to himself, looking puzzled.

An old man wearing plaid Bermuda shorts, a knit shirt, dark socks, and brown leather shoes ran across the sand to confront Velma, Shaggy, and Scooby.

Rich ran over to the group. "It's okay, Mr. Weatherwax, they're with me," he said.

"No dogs allowed," Mr. Weatherwax repeated.

"He's on my property and he'll stay there," Rich said. "You can't tell me who I can and cannot have here. The lighthouse is mine, fair and square. I paid market value for it."

"Darn kids. They'll ruin this place for us all," Weatherwax muttered as he turned and walked toward the ocean.

"I bought the lighthouse from the old guy," Rich explained. "Now he says he wouldn't have sold it to me if he'd known I was going to be bringing crowds in to mess up his beach. I only hope he's right about the crowds."

Rich finally unlocked the door and held it open while everyone filed into the light-house. "You have to have a little imagination to see what it'll be like when I'm finished."

"But you've already got a great music setup here," Velma said, crossing the room toward a stack of equipment on the far side.

"That's not mine," Rich said, glancing at Mike.

"It's mine," Mike admitted. "This place makes a great recording studio. But we're finished now. I came to pick up my equipment before you found it. Too late!" He grinned at his brother.

"Have you . . ." Rich started.

"No, man. I didn't see the pirate again and I never tried to scare anyone away!" Mike insisted.

"Does Cheri's band record here, too?" asked Velma.

"No way. We keep our music separate. I

haven't heard her newest stuff and she hasn't heard mine. It keeps competition to a minimum," Mike said. He leaned over the recording console. "Listen to this." He touched a button and music filled the room.

Daphne hummed along. "Is this original?" she asked, frowning.

"One of our latest, soon-to-be megahits," Mike bragged.

Suddenly, the Motormouths music disappeared, drowned out by the heavy backbeat filling the main room of the lighthouse. A loud guitar lick joined in, ending on a screeching note. Then a shadow fell over the group. It was as if the sun had disappeared. Everyone turned around and looked at the high windows.

"Yikes! It's the pirate! Let's get out of here!" Shaggy yelled. He and Scooby started running toward the door.

"No need," said Daphne. "I think I know who's causing all the trouble."

Do you think you know who's pretending to be the pirate? Turn the page to see if you're right!

"**Y**ou can come down here now, Cheri," Daphne said calmly. "I know you're the pirate."

There was a stunned silence. Then the pirate pulled off its hat and mask, and sure enough, it was Cheri standing up on the balcony.

"Cheri!" Mike said. "But why?"

"Well, at first we thought it was *you* behind the pirate disguise," Fred told him. "I thought perhaps you wanted to keep the lighthouse free for your recording studio."

"And Mr. Weatherwax was a suspect, too," added Velma. "He seemed pretty mad about Rich turning the lighthouse into a club."

"But then I realized that the tape Mike played for us was the same song I'd heard Cheri humming in the truck," Daphne finished. "Right then, I knew it had to be Cheri because she'd told me she and Mike didn't share music. In fact, they didn't even listen to the other's band practice. And Cheri said she was too creeped out to come to the lighthouse. So how would she know the pirate's song unless she'd written it herself?"

When they confronted her, Cheri admitted that she had only pretended to go to the beach, then hurried back, put on her pirate costume, and started the music. She didn't want Mike to find out she was scaring people away from the lighthouse so she could "pirate" his music and record it with her band.

"So, like, there was no pirate?" Shaggy asked.

"Nope, it was just Cheri," said Velma.

"Thanks so much for solving the mystery," said Rich, grabbing each kid's hand and wringing it. "You'll have to come back for the opening night of the club."

"We wouldn't miss it for the world," said Fred, smiling.

"Like, it isn't 'no dogs allowed,' is it?" asked Shaggy, looking worried.

"For Scooby, we'll make an exception," Rich promised.

"Rooby-rooby-roo!" cried Scooby.

"I feel totally underdressed," Daphne said as she looked around at the other guests at the Fashion Extravaganza. "Mr. Bruce didn't say anything about this being a formal event."

"We're dressed in our own unique style," Shaggy said. He and Scooby were sampling appetizers from the long tables set up in the lobby of the design house. "Why are we here, anyway? Not that I'm complaining! The eats are pretty tasty. Right, Scooby?"

"Rum, rum!" Scooby agreed.

A tall, thin woman wearing black gloves

and a long black jacket with black-and-silver buttons over a plain black sheath dress looked at Shaggy and Scooby and wrinkled her nose. "I can't believe you're eating those appetizers. They are full of fat and calories," she said in a haughty voice.

"And they taste good, too," Shaggy said, stuffing another treat into his mouth.

"In case you haven't looked in the mirror lately" — the woman narrowed her eyes and looked Shaggy up and down — "you're growing a bit pudgy around the middle. Not good for the career." She removed her gloves one at a time.

"What career?" Shaggy asked, looking puzzled.

"And your friend," she said, lowering her voice and nodding toward Scooby, "needs to consider laser hair removal."

"I'll tell him," Shaggy said while Fred, Daphne, and Velma stifled their laughter.

"However" — the woman moved closer to Daphne and Fred — "the two of you show possibility. Yes, indeed, you might have a future if you're willing —"

"Daphne! I see you've already met Willow." A bald man dressed completely in black greeted Daphne with a kiss on each cheek.

"Mr. Bruce, they are young and they are beautiful — these two, anyway." Willow pointed to Fred and Daphne with a wave of her glove. "But I don't find a lot of demand for that wholesome corn-fed look. I will see what I can do. My card." Willow handed Daphne and Fred a white card covered with black script.

"Thank you very much, Ms. Willow, but Daphne and I aren't here to try out as models. None of us are," Fred said, turning her card over.

"Willow, please, just Willow," the woman said, fluttering her gloves in Fred's face.

"They're friends of mine, dear," said Mr. Bruce. "They're here to help out" — he cleared his throat — "with a sensitive issue I'm facing."

"Of course, darling, no need to tell me your secrets. I lost that privilege when you told me I was too old and fat to model for you anymore," Willow said sweetly. But her voice was tinged with a tone that told all listeners she didn't mean it to be taken nicely at all.

"Darling! That is not what I said!" Mr. Bruce patted Willow on the shoulder. "I said, and I think I remember the wording exactly, 'I'm changing the look of models that I hire to do my show.'"

"And all the models that you hire are young and extremely thin to the point that I worry about their health," Willow countered.

Mr. Bruce shook his head, still denying Willow's interpretation of her dismissal. "I'm sure you're doing even better with your modeling agency than you did when you worked for me. And all those young men and women who are benefiting from your expert advice! That's worth more than money any day."

Willow rolled her eyes. "I'll be going along now. I'm sure you and your friends have more important things to discuss than me and my career. Ta-ta!" Willow left with a wave over her shoulder, but not before she scooped up several appetizers, wrapped them in a napkin, and stuck them inside her black purse.

"You'll have to forgive Willow," Mr. Bruce said to Daphne and her friends. "She refuses to eat. But being hungry makes her crabby, and then she takes it out on everyone around her."

"That's okay," Shaggy answered. "We won't let these snacks go to waste."

"On to the matter of the day," Mr. Bruce began. "I didn't want to go into detail over the telephone, but I'm in a bit of a fix here and hope you can help me."

"All we know so far is that you've had to cancel two fashion shows," said Velma.

Mr. Bruce nodded. "I have another scheduled for later this afternoon, as you can see, and I don't want another disaster."

"We need to know more about what happened before we'll know whether we can help you or not," Fred said.

"Of course you do! First, I wanted to impress upon you how important it is to have a successful season. My last season, 'Pink and Purple Playfulness,' wasn't as popular with buyers as I'd hoped. If I don't make it up with my 'Red, White, and Blue Spells Summer' collection, I'm afraid I'll be out of business altogether.

"And the competition! Let me tell you, it's brutal. We have to compete just for a mention in the fashion section of the newspaper and *Fashion Fun Daily*, our trade newspaper!"

Velma, Fred, Daphne, Shaggy, and Scooby nodded sympathetically.

"If you'll just tell us . . ." Daphne said.

"I'm getting there. My first show was an evening presentation for out-of-town buyers. My models were dressed and ready to go when this big black thing swooped in and scared them all so much I thought we were going to have to call the paramedics. Two of the girls fainted. It was horrible," Mr. Bruce recounted.

"A big black thing? What do you mean? A bird perhaps?" asked Daphne.

"No. That I could have handled. It was . . ." Mr. Bruce turned red in the face. "It looked like . . . a phantom."

"A fashionable phantom, if it was dressed all in black!" Velma said.

"The same thing happened at our second show. The phantom was the only mention I received in the dailies. I had to hire several new models for this third show because I couldn't get some of the girls to return. And this is my most important show. It simply cannot be ruined!"

An older woman wearing vivid blue eye shadow, bright pink blush, and deep red lipstick rushed up to Mr. Bruce and grabbed his arm. "Bruce, dear, I simply couldn't resist attending your little summer fashion debut!"

"Thank you, Belinda," he said. "Your new season is genius, sheer genius!" Mr. Bruce gushed.

"I hope the buyers agree with you," Belinda said with a giggle. "I love, simply love red, white, and blue in combination. I can see you're busy. Let me find a seat. Toodles!"

The woman rushed away, greeting people right and left.

"Belinda Coffee," Mr. Bruce said with a sigh. "My biggest competition. And it's an unfortunate coincidence that we both chose to feature the same colors this year. She doesn't know it yet, since no one except me and my staff has seen my collection, but she will soon enough."

"What would you like us to do, Mr. Bruce?" Daphne asked.

"I'd like to take you backstage to look around and see if you can find this phantom or some indication of who it is and what it wants from me. I can't afford to cancel another show," said Mr. Bruce, wiping his forehead with his handkerchief.

"Shaggy! Scooby! We're going backstage," Fred said, motioning for them to follow.

"Mr. Bruce," said Shaggy, "you may want to replenish your buffet table. Someone around here has a big appetite." Shaggy and Scooby each carried a heaping plate of appetizers with them as they joined the rest of the gang. The two long tables that had been full of food a few minutes earlier were now almost bare.

"Yes, I'll send someone to see to it," Mr. Bruce said.

"You go ahead and I'll catch up," Daphne told the rest of the gang. She leaned down and picked up a black glove off the floor, then headed toward Willow, who was talking to Belinda Coffee.

As she approached, she heard Willow ask Belinda, "Do you think he had a spy in your showroom? I mean, darling, I've seen his collection and it is so you!"

"You must be mistaken," Belinda replied. "My spies tell me that he is featuring yellow and orange this year, not red, white, and blue."

"Time will tell, won't it, dear?" Willow reached out with one bare arm to tap Belinda's shoulder. "Goodness, it looks like I've . . ."

"Are you looking for this?" Daphne held out the black glove she'd picked up.

"Aren't you the nicest little thing?" said Willow, grabbing the glove from Daphne. She shoved it and its match in her purse. "Thank you." She turned her back to

Daphne and resumed talking with Belinda, this time about models represented by the Willow Agency.

Daphne shrugged, then joined her friends backstage.

Out of the public eye, models were preparing for the upcoming show. Dressers were making last-minute adjustments to the clothes and tension seemed to be running high.

"Being a model doesn't look like as much fun up close as it does in the movies," Velma whispered to Daphne.

Hungry eyes followed Scooby's and Shaggy's plates of appetizers as they walked past waiflike models. "Like, I feel my plate is in danger," Shaggy said to Scooby. One girl reached toward the plate, and the woman helping her dress batted her hand away. "You put on one ounce," the dresser said, "and you won't fit into that hooded red knit dress."

Daphne heard a rustling overhead. She looked up and gasped. A long form wrapped in gauzy black fabric loomed over them. It seemed to float from beam to beam in the mass of catwalks and ropes above their heads. Then, just as quickly as the phantom appeared, it disappeared — but not before Shaggy, Scooby, and several of the models saw it and ran for the exit. Scooby and Shaggy were in the lead.

"My show! Ruined again!" Mr. Bruce cried out. "Girls, girls, come back here right now!" He turned to Daphne, Fred, and Velma. "Can't you do something?"

"I think we should climb up and have a look around," said Fred. "Maybe we'll find a clue that will lead us to the phantom."

"I think I already have a clue, but let's go just to be sure," said Daphne.

A narrow set of stairs led up into the catwalk area. Daphne, Fred, and Velma climbed the stairs, pausing briefly on the landing.

"Hey, guys?" Shaggy's voice called to them from below.

"We're up here!" Fred said.

"We're coming up!" Shaggy and Scooby followed their friends up the stairs.

Daphne, Fred, and Velma headed in separate directions, looking closely at the floor area for clues.

Out of the corner of her eye, Daphne saw something shining. She picked it up and held it out for the others to see.

"Zoinks! Look behind you!" Shaggy said in a shaky voice. "It's the phantom!"

"No need to be scared. This is just what I needed to prove my suspicions," Daphne announced.

Do you think you know who's behind the fashionable phantom? Turn the page to see if you're right!

Fred and Shaggy reached out and pulled the phantom as it began to float by them. It was wrapped completely in black and suspended by wires from the catwalks. The phantom resisted, but quickly became so tangled in its gauzy cloth that it gave up, stumbling to the catwalk floor.

Mr. Bruce had joined the gang on the catwalk, breathless from his run up the stairs. "You caught the phantom!" he gasped. "I just knew you would. Who is it?"

"Willow," Daphne declared, brushing the yards of fabric from the phantom's face.

It was indeed Willow, looking very put out.

"Initially, we picked out three people we believed might have a reason to want to 'haunt' your fashion show," Velma began. "They were you yourself, Mr. Bruce, for the attention it would bring your collection; Belinda, because she wanted to eliminate the competition; and Willow, because she wanted revenge on you for firing her as one of your models."

108

"Then Willow became a prime candidate when she mentioned to Belinda that Mr. Bruce's collection was red, white, and blue," Daphne continued. "But you had said that no one but your staff had seen the new line."

"No one but your staff — and the phantom," Fred put in. "Because of the phantom, all your shows had been canceled. So no one had seen any of your new clothes."

"We knew for sure when I found a silver-and-black button on the catwalk. It had to be Willow," Daphne finished.

"And I would've gotten away with it, too, if it weren't for you meddling kids and your dog," Willow growled.

"Kids, how can I ever thank you?" Mr. Bruce exclaimed. "Wait . . . I'm having an idea. . . ."

Minutes later, Fred, Daphne, Velma, and Shaggy walked onstage to thunderous applause. They were dressed in red, white, and blue garments from Mr. Bruce's new collection.

"They look fabulous!" cried a reporter in the crowd.

"So healthy, so young and fresh, so . . . *American*," gushed another.

Then Scooby bounded onstage, a bandanna that looked like an American flag wrapped around his neck. He stopped and struck a pose next to his friends, who gathered around him. "Rooby-rooby-roo!" cried Scooby.

"It's really great of you guys to come with me and my cousin, Ferd, on his first day of summer school," said Fred.

"This is a different school from the one I usually go to," Ferd explained. He paused for a second, gulping. "And I've heard some scary stories about it."

"You know how exaggerated stories can become," Velma tried to reassure him.

Ferd's hands were clasped so tightly in his lap his knuckles were white. "I also heard that the school is haunted."

"Have a bite to eat, Ferd. You may need it." Shaggy stuck a bag of chips over the seat.

Ferd ignored the offer of chips, but Scooby grabbed a pawful and snarfed them down.

"Kids said the school I went to was haunted, too, but it was a made-up story." Daphne patted Ferd on the shoulder.

"Th — thanks for coming along, Daphne," Ferd said, looking up at her adoringly.

"My pleasure, Ferd." Daphne smiled warmly at the boy, who was like a younger, smaller version of Fred.

"What's for lunch at summer school?" Shaggy asked. "The best thing about school is lunch, right, Scooby?"

"Right," Scooby agreed.

"Classes are only in the morning," said Ferd. "This is a special program with kids from all over town. We're supposed to get to do fun stuff like launch rockets and make models."

"Maybe we should stay," said Shaggy. "It sounds pretty cool."

Fred pulled the Mystery Machine up in front of the brick school. "We'll walk you inside," he told Ferd, climbing out of the van.

"Thanks." Ferd jumped out and held the door for Daphne and Velma. "We're supposed to meet in the front hallway for a tour. Maybe you can come along."

But as the gang and Ferd headed up the front steps, they were almost run over by a group of screaming schoolchildren racing out the doors.

"Come back here right now!" a short, plump woman wearing a navy blue suit called after the runaways. "I insist you return to the building this minute."

"What's with the wild bunch?" Shaggy asked, pointing over his shoulder at the fleeing kids.

"They're scared of " — the woman glanced at Ferd, whose eyes had grown huge at the sight of the running kids — "something. You know how children can be." She laughed nervously. "I'm Ms. Bledsoe, the principal. Don't believe the stories that my school is haunted."

113

"I — I'm Ferd and I'm here for summer classes," Fred's cousin said.

"Perhaps you can show your friends around the school, Ferd, while I . . . well, I have a few things to take care of." Ms. Bledsoe pulled open the office door and disappeared inside.

"If the school isn't haunted," Ferd said, "why did everyone run away like that?"

"Maybe we should ask them," Velma suggested.

The kids had stopped at the curb and were looking back at the school, talking among themselves. Velma led Ferd and the gang to talk to them.

"Hi, guys!" Fred greeted them. "We felt like we were going the wrong way on a one-way street back there. What's up?"

The kids just looked at one another. Finally, a thin, dark-haired boy wearing round glasses and braces stepped forward. "This school is haunted. My big brother, Robbie, said it was and my mom told me he was making it all up. But what happens as soon as we get inside?" He paused. "We hear a ghost and almost get attacked by a big old bird!"

"Roger is right," said a tall girl with long red pigtails. "It was like the ghost was everywhere at once. '*Whoooooo*,' it moaned, '*whooooo's in my hallway?*'" She shivered.

"No, Carrie, you're wrong. It went, '*Booooooo, gooooooo awaaaaaay*,'" Roger said. Carrie, the girl with red hair, folded her arms across her chest and glared down at Roger.

"You're both wrong!" interrupted a girl with curly blond hair. "It said, '*Mooooooove, moooooove awaaaaaay*' — like we were getting too close to it. Then the bird came flying over us. I was afraid it was going to land right on my head." Her eyes filled with tears.

Ferd moved closer to Daphne and took her hand.

"The bird probably flew in an open door or window and was trying to find its way out," said Velma. "It was probably more frightened than you."

"And it looks like there's some disagreement on what the ghost was trying to tell

115

you guys. Could it have possibly been some-one testing the PA system?" Fred asked.

Again, the kids exchanged looks. A few nodded, others shrugged.

"What if we go inside, take a look around, and make sure there's nothing there?" Fred said.

"No way!" said Shaggy.

"Ro ray!" echoed Scooby.

"How else are you going to find the cafe-teria?" Velma asked.

"We are out of snacks, Scoob," Shaggy said.

"Then come with us," said Daphne. She turned to the kids standing by the road. "We'll send Ms. Bledsoe out to talk to you. She's pretty upset at losing her students be-fore the day even started."

"I'll come, too," Ferd volunteered. "Daphne might need someone to protect her."

"No need to worry . . ." Fred started. Daphne caught Fred's glance and shook her head. "Okay, Ferd, come with us. Any other volunteers?"

Almost as one, the kids shook their heads.

"I want to call my mother," Carrie said. "I don't care if I might get to be in a stupid movie and be discovered and turn out to be famous. I want to go home!"

"We'll have to let Ms. Bledsoe make that decision," said Velma. "You guys wait here while we go make sure it's safe for you to come back inside."

The gang walked back inside the school. Fred knocked on the door of the office.

Ms. Bledsoe opened it. "Yes? Did you convince my students to come back inside?"

"Not yet," Fred told her, "but we're going to take a look around the building."

"Will you keep a lookout for Pepe?" asked Ms. Bledsoe. She pointed to a large, empty birdcage. "The student who fed him this morning must not have latched the door tightly enough and he got out. Poor birdie, he'll be so frightened."

"That explains part of what scared your students," said Velma. "You may want to go out and tell them about Pepe." Velma pointed at the tight knot of children waiting at the curb.

"The children? My summer school children?" Ms. Bledsoe clapped her hands. "Thank you for bringing them back!" She grabbed Scooby's paw, then Shaggy's hand, and pumped it up and down eagerly. "I may not have to turn over my school to Mr. McCall after all." The principal ran outside and joined the group.

"Who is Mr. McCall?" Fred asked.

"He's the principal at my regular school. It's a lot smaller than this one," said Ferd. "I think he's going to teach a class here this summer. He's pretty cool. Every year he makes a videotape of us when we start school and then shows it to us at the end of the year. He makes it so good, it's almost like watching a movie."

"I bet it is," said Daphne.

"Let's split up and see what's going on here. Shaggy, you and Scooby go that way" — Fred pointed down a set of steps — "and see what's down there. Maybe it's the cafeteria."

"Okay, Scooby, the last one to find the cafeteria has to pay. Deal?" said Shaggy.

"Real!" Scooby and Shaggy exchanged high fives. They took off.

"The kids came from this direction." Fred started to walk down a long, dark hall, followed by Ferd, Daphne, and Velma. Their footsteps echoed in the empty school.

"I don't hear anything. Do you hear anything?" Ferd whispered.

"Just us," said Velma.

There was a loud click, then a sound like someone blowing in a microphone. "Testing, testing," a voice came over the loudspeaker.

"We know the loudspeaker works!" said Fred.

"It's Mr. McCall," said Ferd. "He loves to talk over the loudspeaker. Our school probably has more morning announcements than any other school in the world."

"Wait a minute!" Daphne stopped and put her finger over her lips. "I think I hear something down this way." She pointed down a shorter hallway.

The sound of laughter drifted toward them and grew louder as they approached the classroom at the end of the hall.

Fred rapped on the door a couple of times, then opened it. "What's going on in here?" he asked.

A group of kids was standing around a TV. "Your brother . . ." the only girl in the group began. But she stopped talking as soon as she saw Fred, Daphne, Velma, and Ferd.

The three students, two boys and the girl, all older than Ferd, turned away from the television screen they'd been watching. There was a click, then the screen went dark and a videocassette popped out of the VCR.

"Are you teachers?" the tallest of the group, a dark-haired boy, asked.

"Robbie, they aren't old enough to be teachers. Besides, that one is too cute!" The girl smiled at Fred, flashing her dimples.

"We were having a look around your school," Fred said. "Did you guys hear anything strange a little while ago? See anything?" he asked.

The three students shook their heads. "Why?" asked Robbie. He zipped and unzipped a black bag resting in his lap.

120

Fred turned to Daphne, Velma, and Ferd. "See, I was right. It was just the loudspeaker system. And the bird was Ms. Bledsoe's Pepe."

A very tall man with a graying beard barged into the classroom. "Show time!" he said. "I'll go get —"

Robbie interrupted him. "Mr. McCall, these people are looking around the school for Pepe. And they also said some of the kids heard strange noises."

Mr. McCall stroked his beard. "Right, the PA. We all remarked upon the strangeness of those noises when they occurred."

"We'd better find Ferd's classroom before he's late," said Fred.

"Ferd!" Mr. McCall clapped Ferd on the back. "Good to see you, man. I think you're going to get a kick out of summer school."

"I'm glad you're here, too, sir," said Ferd.

"I'm sure I'll see you later. Have fun!" Mr. McCall ushered them out of the classroom and shut the door behind them.

"Let's find Scooby and Shaggy," said Fred. "I think I may know what's going on here."

The group retraced their route back toward the front of the school. In the main hallway, Fred made a side trip to the office. He ran his finger down a list of classes, then nodded.

The gang found Scooby and Shaggy sitting on the front steps.

"The cafeteria is locked up tight," Shaggy said sadly. "No chili mac, no tuna surprise, no grilled cheese, none of those gourmet treats."

"Did you find anything else?" asked Fred.

"We were too depressed to look any further," said Shaggy.

"Let's have a look now," said Fred.

"It's dark down there," Shaggy warned.

Lights flickered as they walked toward the cafeteria. Then a low buzz sounded, seeming to fill the space around them. It grew into a hum, then a moan.

"Scooby-Doo, let's get out of here!" Shaggy was up the stairs before Fred could stop him.

Ferd grabbed Fred's hand and squeezed.

"Nothing to worry about," said Fred. "But

check your hair and makeup and smile, because . . ." Fred's voice trailed off just as a
bright light switched on ahead of them.

Do you think you know what's causing the mysterious events at Ferd's school? Turn the page to see if
you're right!

"Why is that light shining on us?" Ferd cried, blocking his eyes.

"Because you're on candid camera," Fred said, laughing. "I pieced together several clues and figured out that the older students were making a scary movie as part of one of their courses."

"Rhat? Really?" cried Scooby, his head poking around the corner.

"A scary movie? Is Mr. McCall helping them?" Ferd didn't look scared anymore — now he looked excited!

"That's right, Ferd," Daphne said, bending down to hug the young boy. "Remember, one of the students outside mentioned she wanted to go home even though she might get to be in a movie."

"That's right," said Velma. "Then the three older students were watching a tape that they clicked off as soon as we came into the room. They didn't want us to know what they were up to."

"And another student was holding a camera bag. The students said they hadn't

124

heard anything strange earlier, yet Mr. McCall said they'd all remarked upon the strange noises," Fred continued.

"Plus, you'd already told us that Mr. McCall was a whiz with a video camera, making him a logical choice to teach the class," Daphne said, smiling at Ferd.

"The rest of the summer school students — and Ms. Bledsoe's bird, Pepe — are the unsuspecting stars of a movie being made by Mr. McCall's video class!" Velma declared.

"We'd better go tell her what's going on before she worries anymore," said Fred.

"Reah, ret's ro," agreed Scooby.

"But, like, as long as we're down here, we might as well get some snacks, right?" asked Shaggy.

Velma laughed. "I can't believe you guys want to eat cafeteria food. Now I know you guys really *will* eat anything!"

Ferd, Fred, and Daphne laughed along with her. Scooby and Shaggy just shrugged — and headed for the snacks.

"**T**his is our idea of a good time, right, Scooby?" Shaggy said. The two friends sniffed the fairground air, which was heavy with the smell of barbecue. "When do we eat?"

"There you are, Shaggy! I didn't think you'd miss the barbecue cook-off!" A small red-haired woman wearing a stained apron grabbed Shaggy and Scooby and pulled them toward a small booth in a long line of identical booths.

"Guys, this is Cindy Lane. She runs Barbie's Q, where Scoob and I sometimes eat," Shaggy introduced his friend to Velma, Fred, and Daphne.

"Sometimes?" Cindy laughed. "They're my best customers!"

"What's the drill here?" Fred asked, looking around at the barbecue grills set up in front of the booths.

"You buy a ticket, then visit each cook and try their barbecue. After you've visited all of them, you vote for your favorite. It's a great honor to be voted best barbecue in town," Cindy explained.

"Where do you get the tickets?" asked Velma.

"You guys are my guests," said Cindy, reaching into her apron pocket and pulling out tickets for everyone.

"We get to go to each booth once?" asked Shaggy.

"Shaggy, there must be twenty different kinds of barbecue to try here!" Daphne exclaimed.

"If you're still hungry, I have a couple of extra tickets," Cindy said.

"Let's get started!" Shaggy said, grabbing

his ticket. "We'll be back in a while, Cindy. We're going to save the best for last!"

"Rest ror rast," Scooby said with a nod.

"I figured I could count on your votes at least — as long as I got you to show up," said Cindy. "I need to win this contest or I don't know how much longer I can stay open." Cindy turned back to her grill and flipped the burgers. She brushed more sauce over the patties as she waved the smoke away.

"Thanks for the tickets," Daphne called to Cindy as they moved to the neighboring booth.

"Welcome to Veggie-Q," the young man standing over the grill said. "I guarantee this is the tastiest and healthiest barbecue you'll find anywhere." He served each one of the gang a barbecue veggie burger on a whole-wheat bun.

Shaggy and Scooby ate theirs in two bites, consulted, then Shaggy made notes on a pad he pulled out of his pocket.

"You're pretty serious about this," the cook said.

"They take their food very seriously," Velma said.

"I'm Andy Shaw." The man held out his hand.

Velma reached for it, but Andy pulled it back and wiped it on his apron, then offered it again. "Sorry about that," Andy said. "Cooking can get a little messy. If you're not in the mood for a veggie burger, I have some barbecue veg-kabobs on my back grill."

"We'd better try those," Shaggy said, holding out his plate for some.

Daphne, Velma, and Fred shared a veg-kabob.

"That was good," said Fred, wiping barbecue sauce off his mouth.

"Different," Daphne said.

"My barbecue sauce contains all-natural ingredients and no meat by-products," Andy called after them as they walked to the next booth.

Daphne, Velma, and Fred could barely keep up with Shaggy and Scooby as they ate their way through the cook-off.

"Do you like it?" the cook at Richard

O'Ribs asked nervously. "Do you think the sauce is too sweet? Is it too spicy? What's wrong with it?"

Daphne nibbled on the barbecued ribs he handed her. "It's good," she assured him.

"It's an old family recipe," the man said. "This is the first time my dad, the original Richard, has trusted me to mix the sauce myself. I'm Rich Junior, but everyone calls me Junior. I guess I'm worried I'll let him down. Dad has won the cook-off for the past five years. He'd be here today, but he had a heart attack and is still in the hospital. I don't want to let him down. Want another taste?" Junior held out more BBQ sauce.

"We're fine," said Fred.

"I might need just one more," Shaggy said, tasting the sauce and sharing with Scooby.

"I'm stuffed," said Velma as they moved on. "And all the barbecue sauce is starting to taste the same," she whispered.

Daphne and Fred agreed. "Let's go over and listen to the band for a while and give our stomachs a rest," Velma suggested.

"But what if they run out of food?" Shaggy asked.

"Ladies and gentlemen!" a voice came over the loudspeaker. "May I have your attention for a moment? We are very pleased to welcome country music legend Patsy Hill and her Cowboy Band to the cook-off. Our cooks have been so busy that they'd like to have a few moments to fix up a new batch of barbecue for you to enjoy. Plus, the way some of you have been eating, I'm thinking you'd better rest for a few minutes or you'll wear out your jaws with all the chewing!"

Shaggy and Scooby nodded and massaged their jaws.

"All of you come over here for a spell and listen to Miss Patsy Hill," the announcer finished.

The crowd started to drift over to the stage that had been set up for entertainment. Patsy Hill and her band warmed up, then broke into the chorus of her latest hit, "You Left Me Alone with a Broken Heart and Busted Plumbing."

"That's a strange drumbeat," said Velma

as a steady *bud-a-bum, bud-a-bum, bud-a-bum* almost drowned out Patsy's singing.

"It's not even close to the tune of the song," Daphne agreed.

Just then, there was a loud cracking sound, followed by yells and shouts. The music stopped and everyone turned in the direction of the shouts.

The booths were collapsing like a row of dominoes as a white cow with big, sharp horns ran amok! It reared up on its hind legs and pulled at the canvas sheeting of the booths. The contestants ran out of the booths and watched, horrified, as their grills, vats, and bowls of sauce mixed with dust.

The gang from Mystery, Inc., minus Shaggy and Scooby, ran to the cook-off area to see what had happened.

"My sauce!" Cindy Lane cried. "All my supplies!"

"I'll never be able to make as good a batch of sauce as that one," Junior moaned.

"We'll help you clean up, Cindy," Fred volunteered. "The cook-off's not over yet."

Daphne and Fred pulled the canvas away from the spot where Cindy's booth had stood. Cindy was on the verge of tears as she surveyed the mess. "I put the last of my savings into supplies for this cook-off. I bought the highest grade beef available, the best ingredients for my sauce, hickory wood chips to add flavor. And it's all gone just because of a stupid cow."

Andy joined them, wiping sweat from his forehead. "Did you see that?" he demanded. "Did you see what happened?"

"You mean the cow?" asked Velma.

"A huge white bull ran right over our booths, knocking everything into the dirt. Where did it come from?" Andy stared open-mouthed at the mess the cook-off had become.

"The cow?" said Shaggy, joining the group. "Like, maybe it was protesting all the beef that's being eaten here today."

"Not a cow, that was a bull, like I told you. Only bulls have horns. And how would you feel if you saw a bunch of bulls eating people?" Andy asked, looking serious.

Shaggy's mouth opened and closed, but no words came out.

"All I've got to say is, you'd all better take this as a warning and change your eating habits before that bull talks other bulls and cows into joining it on its crusade." Andy walked off.

"Someone's cow must have gotten out by accident," Daphne said.

"But how did a cow get all the way out here?" Velma asked.

"A bull, not a cow," Shaggy reminded them. "Who knows? Bad luck," he added with a shrug.

Velma looked more closely at the hoof-prints in the dirt. She followed them the length of the row. She passed contestants trying to salvage their supplies, but few were finding much left.

In the parking lot, Velma ran into Andy, who was hauling unopened boxes of veggie burgers toward the fairground.

"Look at that trailer over there." Andy lifted his chin toward what looked like a horse trailer. "Still wonder how the bull got out here?"

The red-and-white-checked horse trailer had *Barbie's Q* written across it in fancy black script.

Daphne caught up with Velma in the parking lot. "What are you doing? We're going into town to see if we can buy more supplies for Cindy."

"Come over here for a minute," Velma said. She led Daphne toward the trailer. Velma stood on her toes to look inside, and it was neat as a pin. The floor was shiny and clean, and cooking equipment was neatly stored on shelves built into the walls.

"Doesn't look like there's been any animals inside there for a while," said Daphne. "I know Cindy said she needed to win this cook-off, but I don't think she'd stoop to this level to do it."

"Where could the cow be?" Velma mused.

Daphne shrugged. The girls walked back to Cindy's booth.

"Here you go, have a barbecued veggie

burger. All-natural ingredients in my sauce, healthier and tastier than anything else around here," Andy was saying as they passed his booth. Shaggy and Scooby were at the head of the line, and most of the other people at the fair were behind them.

"The horse trailer?" Cindy said when Velma asked her. "That's how I carry my catering supplies to party sites," she said. "I guess it does look odd, but you can go inside and see that it's clean." Again she looked on the verge of tears.

"Did you see where the cow went after it knocked everything down?" asked Velma.

Cindy shook her head. Velma made another trip down the row of booths, asking contestants the same question, but no one remembered seeing hide nor hair of the bull after it knocked down the booths.

"I think I know where it might be," Velma announced.

Do you know where the bull is? See the next page to find out if you're right!

"Come on, gang, I've got a plan," said Velma, beckoning her friends to her. She huddled with Fred, Daphne, Shaggy, and Scooby for a few minutes, then the group broke apart.

"Do you know what to do, Shaggy?" Velma asked.

"Sure!" Shaggy declared. "I'd do anything to help Cindy."

"Re, roo." Scooby nodded.

Shaggy and Scooby walked up to Andy's booth. "Like, do you mind if we borrow some of your supplies for Cindy?" Shaggy asked.

"Sure, go ahead," Andy said distractedly. He was busy serving his still-long line of customers.

Shaggy and Scooby started poking around in Andy's booth. But when Scooby picked up a big box that had been hastily shoved in the corner, Andy turned and yelled, "No! Stay away from that!"

But it was too late. Scooby had already found the bull costume inside.

"Just as I thought," Velma said, joining her friends.

Cindy was right behind her. "But how did you know?" she gasped.

"Well, I followed the hoofprints as far as the parking lot, where I ran into Andy bringing in fresh supplies. He was the only contestant to have anything extra on hand — almost as if he knew he was going to need it."

"We also suspected Junior, who had a good motive — he was worried he would let his dad down by not winning the competition."

"And we thought it might be you, Cindy, when we saw your trailer. But we couldn't think of a reason why you would do it."

"Oh, I would never do anything like this!" Cindy exclaimed. "But why did you, Andy?"

"Barbecuing beef is wrong! I had to strike a blow for vegetarianism," Andy declared.

"Well, even though your motives may not have been bad, we're still going to have to turn you in to the judges," Fred said firmly. He led Andy off to the judges' stand.

"Don't worry, Cindy, you're definitely going to win — at least if me and Scooby have anything to say about it!" Shaggy pulled out his notepad and showed it to Cindy. "You were the only barbecue chef to score over a 9.5 in all possible areas — spiciness, tastiness, tenderness . . ." Shaggy continued to read from his notes as Cindy, Daphne, and Velma just laughed.

"Rooby-rooby-roo!" cried Scooby.